TEARS FOR A COPPER

TEARS FOR A COPPER

RUSSELL WILLIAMS

NAVIGATOR BOOKS

Published by Navigator Books
Ringwood, Hampshire

ISBN 0 902830 19 8

This book is a work of fiction and no resemblance to actual places or persons living or dead is to be inferred. Any such resemblance would be entirely coincidental.

Typeset by Moorhouse Typesetters
Printed by The Cromwell Press, Melksham, Wiltshire.

To my mother, Kathleen (Nee Russell-Williams)
for all she meant to me and to my wife, Molly,
and our daughters - for fulfilling my life.

Chapter 1

The break came just as Bell was getting ready to go off duty at five o'clock. The telephone rang and he was nearest to it. Absent-mindedly he picked up the receiver and announced that the caller was through to C.I.D.

"Who would you like to speak to?", he asked, looking around the squad office.

"Anyone will do", said the voice on the telephone.

It was a gruff voice, and there was a touch of urgency to its tone.

"Alright", Bell replied, "I'm anyone, what's your problem?".

"Right", said the voice. "Listen carefully. You know about the warehouse breakings don't you? Well, Harvey and Brown's are gonna get done tonight. Radios and tape gear. Dunno what time and I ain't gonna tell you who it will be. There will be two of 'em though, wiv a grey van. They're goin' over the back wall".

"How do you know all this?", asked Bell, getting interested.

"Look, I know, okay?", replied the gruff voice. "I just want to see 'em copped".

"Can you tell me who you are?", asked Bell, "can I meet you somewhere?".

"No" said the voice, "Not this time. This one's for me own satisfaction". There was a click and the line went dead.

Bell replaced the receiver and stood thoughtfully for some seconds. He had worked on the warehouse jobs himself, or at least, half of them, and he would like to see the villains inside. Recently more than a dozen warehouses had been attacked, and property worth half a million pounds had been stolen. The methods suggested that the same people were responsible for all the crimes. Up to the day, the C.I.D. had nothing to go on in their hunt for information; but at last, a chink of light shone through the barrier of silence.

The Chief Inspector's door opened, and the guv'nor walked out with a large bundle of papers in his hand.

"Sir", said Bell, walking away from the telephone, a message sheet in his hand. "Have you got a minute please?".

"What is it Bell?", the Chief Inspector said impatiently, "I've got to get these despatches away before the Admin closes".

"Well, I'd better hang on and have a word with you after then, Sir", said Bell, "It's very important".

"Alright", said the Chief Inspector, "I won't be more than five minutes". He hurried out of the door.

Bell sat on the edge of his desk and started to imagine the layout of Harvey and Brown's warehouse. He had been there a couple of times before, when there had been a spate of thefts from employee's cars in the car park. He visualised the high wall, some ten feet above the ground and the wide car park surrounded by high and thick bushes.

"Ideal for obbo's", he thought.

He took a sheet of paper and drew the layout from memory, indicating the line of bushes and the approximate distance across the car park. There were some double loading doors leading into the warehouse on the other side of the wall, about halfway along; and windows every twelve feet or so. He put it all on paper.

"Now then Bell", the Chief Inspector said, returning to his office, "come on in".

Bell followed Detective Chief Inspector Frost into his office. Frost took his seat and waved a hand at another chair the other side of his desk. Bell sat down and crossed his long legs.

"It's about the warehouse breaks, Sir", he began.

"What about them?", asked Frost. "Have you got a lead yet?".

"I think so, Sir", replied Bell. "I've just had an anonymous tip off that Harvey and Brown's are going to be done tonight, for radios and tape recorders".

Frost sat up and showed immediate interest.

"Very good", he said, eyes widening and a hint of a smile lighting up his serious face. "What time?".

"Ah, well that's the problem Sir", retorted Bell. "We don't know".

"Is the informant reliable?", Frost asked, always suspicious of such information. "Has he given you information before?".

"I don't know him Sir", said Bell, "and I can't say I could place his voice".

The Chief was silent for a moment. He seemed to be chewing over the information and sorting it out in his mind. At last he looked up and smiled.

"You'll have to do observations yourself then", he announced - "all night".

Bell sagged. He had guessed that he would end up with observations on this job, but he had half hoped that someone else would have got the job instead.

"Well don't look so damned happy about it", Frost barked. "What else do you expect? I can't put my night duty men on it".

"Alright Sir", said Bell, feeling miserable at the prospects of a long night. "Who's available to come with me Sir".

Frost consulted his duty board. "You'd better take young Peterson", he said. "Take the Consul and a couple of radios. Make a start at eight o'clock. Good luck".

"Thank you", said Bell, standing and making towards the door, "I'll brief the uniform people myself before I start".

"Right", replied Frost. "Let them know what they can expect".

Bell walked out of the office and into the large room which was furnished with desks lined up along each wall and along the centre.

"Anyone seen Peterson?", he called. About half a dozen Detectives sat at their desks, writing up reports. There was no reply. "Don't all answer at once", Bell said, pocketing the message he still held in his hand. He stormed out of the door and made towards the canteen.

Peterson was draped across the canteen counter. He was dressed, as usual in a sharp looking grey suit that must have cost him a lot of money. He was a good dresser and led the way in fashion amongst his colleagues.

"Bill", called Bell. "What are you on?"

Peterson looked around. "Hello Harry, thought you had gone off", he said.

"So did I", Bell replied. "What are you on?"

"I'm off at ten", Peterson said, "got a few calls to make later on, but nothing much".

"Good", Bell said. "You'd better get them done early then - you're on all night with me".

"Come off it", chided Peterson, "doing what?"

"We're on obbo's all night. See you here at seven thirty sharp. You'd better get yourself a flask and something to eat. It wouldn't be a bad idea if you got something warm to wear too".

"But I have a date at ten o'clock", moaned Peterson "right cracker she is too".

"Hard luck", laughed Bell. "You'd better put her on ice then".

Bell walked away and out to the car park where he unlocked his own car, a rather beat-up Austin.

"Time I changed this old bomb for something a bit more up to date", he thought as he climbed in. The car park was full and he realised, to his disgust, that his car was the oldest-looking one there. He reversed out of his space and hit the road, driving thoughtlessly as he headed out of town towards his home. Another evening spoiled, another row with his wife was inevitable. More words, more suspicions, more explanations. That was the unfortunate lot of a Detective these days. No time to call your own.

A big black dog ran across the road in front of him, causing him to swerve and brake hard. The dog ran on, unharmed. "Bloody dogs", Bell shouted "never ought to be allowed in towns". He thought about the black dog and a smile broke the stern frown. "Funny", he thought "how many police cars have been involved in accidents because of some 'big black, mysterious dog', that always gets away". He chuckled. "Wouldn't it be a laugh if someone were to capture such a dog and clear up all the accidents still outstanding".

He drove on and cursed the traffic, always thick and always driven on by hundreds of maniacs, caring nothing for the other chap. He took the opportunity of shooting into the roundabout as the traffic slowed and a motorcyclist appeared from nowhere and almost ended up in the side of Bell's car. The coarse exchange of words that followed was inevitable.

Bell completed the rest of his short journey in comparative safety.

"Dinner's in the oven", Susan Bell called from upstairs as she heard her husband come in. "I'll be down in a minute".

Bell went to the kitchen and rinsed his hands under a scalding hot tap. He dried them on the kitchen towel and opened the oven door. A roast dinner greeted him and raised his spirits a little. At least he could always expect a good meal when he came home. He sat down to eat and a few minutes later, Sue came down and joined him. She was a good-looking woman with long dark hair. She had a soft voice and a good figure. They had been married for five years, and although she had got used to his unpredictable hours she didn't like the sudden jobs that always ruined her arrangements.

"Like the new dress?", she said, twirling around like a mannequin. "I bought it today".

"Nice", said Bell, chewing a piece of beef.

"I thought we might go out somewhere tonight, Harry", she said. "Somewhere nice and quiet, for a drink. We could try that new place just out of town, you know, the place you were telling me about last night".

Bell felt sickened. "Here it comes", he thought. "Sorry love", he said "I'm back on duty at seven thirty".

"Oh, now Harry, you've just done all day, surely you're not going to expect me to believe that you are going back on duty again".

"Yes", said Bell. "All night".

"What!" Sue shouted, "you can't be serious".

"I'm afraid so", said Bell, mouth full of green beans - "observations".

"But what's wrong with someone else?" she said half sobbing. "Why you?" Her voice faltered.

"That's how it goes", said Bell. "Besides, it was on my information. I am involved with the job anyway, and what's more, there isn't anyone else to spare".

"So they can just detail you off to do all day and all night", she said, "just like that".

"Just like that", Bell echoed tonelessly.

"What's the job then?", Sue challenged.

"Warehouse-break", he replied.

"What warehouse?"

"Does it really matter?", he barked, getting annoyed. He hated to be quizzed by his wife as if he were doing something wrong. "Why?", he thought, "should I have to justify myself every time something like this came up".

"How do I know it's not just and excuse for you being with another woman?", she sneered, unreasonably.

"You don't", said Bell softly, "but if it's any use to you, I'm taking young Bill Peterson with me".

"That's even more reason to suspect illicit affairs then", said Sue. "I know of his reputation".

Bell pushed the remainder of the meal way. He was thoroughly miserable and didn't want to row with Sue. He loved her and always had. He had given her no valid reason to suspect that he was philandering. Sure, he met other women, lots of them - beautiful women. But that was all part of the job. He didn't take advantage of the situation, although he had been given plenty of opportunity in that direction.

"Sue", he said. "I'm on duty tonight. I shall be sitting in a Police car in the company of another Detective. We shall be watching a warehouse for villains. With any luck, they will come and we may arrest them. On the other hand, they may not come. Whatever happens, I shall be out there, on the job, not in some other woman's bed. Alright?"

Sue was silent. She looked at her husband and saw a tired man. He had aged in the past few years. Detective work had demanded much of his time and his sleep. He had become hard and cynical and to some extent, bitter. The system had not done him a lot of good and promotion never seemed to be within his grasp. However, he never allowed it to interfere with his work. Villains were his problem and he did his best to catch them. His methods were perhaps, sometimes a little unorthodox, but then, the villains didn't think twice about the methods they adopted, right or wrong.

She softened and went over to him, slipping her hands round his neck from behind. He sat still, wanting to hold his wife in his arms; but her attitude had made him even bitter towards her when she carried on like this. "I'm sorry darling", she said, kissing his ear. "I don't really mistrust you. It's just that I feel so disappointed when you have to go back on duty, or when you don't come home on time. I miss you, Harry..... and I love you".

Bell swung round in his chair and put his arms around his wife's waist as he buried his head in her bosom.

"Sure", he murmured, "I know".

Sue bent forward and touched his lips with hers.

"Be careful", she said, a tear rolling from her eye.

"I will", Bell replied, "don't worry about me".

An hour later, flask of coffee and a bundle of sandwiches in his briefcase, Bell headed back towards the town centre and the Police Station. The town was less busy now and gangs of youths wandered the darkened streets, shouting and catcalling. Later, the street would be occupied by the prostitutes and the drunks. Junkies would hang about the public toilets, hoping to be able to buy a fix or trade in unwanted pills.

"Back again then Harry", the Station Sergeant queried as Bell walked into the quiet enquiry office.

Sergeant Jones was an old hand with twenty-five years service in the Force. He was due for retirement. His days of playing the hard line were over and he treated everyone with the same degree of respect.

"Obbo job tonight, Serge", Bell said. "All night".

He briefed the Sergeant and the Inspector and told them exactly where he proposed to position his car. He asked that uniform activities be kept to an absolute minimum in the area for fear of frightening off the villains.

"If we should shout for assistance though", he went on, "we'd like it fast".

"You'll get it", Sergeant Jones said.

"Thanks", Bell nodded, and he went off to find Peterson.

Chapter 2

Harry Bell settled back into the leather upholstery of the dark green Ford Consul and lit another cigarette. He eased his cramped legs to recirculate the blood which had almost ceased to flow after several hours of sitting in one position. He blew smoke through the open window, and sighed.

Bell was a tall man, slimly built and thirty years old. He had been in the Police Force for ten years, and during that time had become accustomed to long hours of waiting and watching. It was part of his job; not perhaps, the part that he liked best, not by any means, but just the same, part of the job as a Detective. Sometimes observations paid off; mostly though, they dwindled out after many fruitless hours, and another informant would be marked with a query.

Alongside him, Bill Peterson relaxed with his head against the door pillar. He was younger, about twenty-five, agile and rather more athletic than Bell. A good looking man and single, his conversation often turned to women. He was rarely short of the company of beautiful girls, and he liked to boast of his conquests.

The night was dark, and a hint of moonlight showed from time to time between the darkening clouds which blackened the sky. The breeze stirred the litter in the car park,and the sound of papers scudding across the ground, caused the men to keep their eyes glued to the area around them. They were well concealed behind a large cluster of rhododendron bushes, and the only part of their car which was exposed, was the front, affording them a clear view of the warehouse on the other side of the car park. A high brick wall skirted the rear of the building which contained several thousands of pounds worth of radios and tape recorders.

"What time is it?", Peterson yawned, stretching languidly, as far as the confines of the car would allow.

"Twelve fifteen", said Bell, studying his watch face in the light of a cigarette.

"Christ!", said Peterson, opening the door and getting out, "I'm bursting".

"Don't bang the door", said Bell, quietly.

Peterson closed the door and stood in the bushes. A few seconds passed then.

"Did you hear that?".....it was Peterson, his face framed in the open window of the car door.

"Hear what?", asked Bell.

"A bang", said Peterson, "sounded like it came from the far end of the building".

Both men looked towards the far end of the warehouse and listened.

"Can you get around that side?", asked Bell. "I'm bloody sure you can't get a van around there".

They were both silent, ears straining for the slightest sound.

"Was that glass breaking?", Bell said, almost to himself.

"Could have been", whispered Peterson.

"Come on then", Bell said. "Quietly as you can, follow the bushes and keep in the shadows. We'll see what's going on round there".

Together they crept in the shadows. Bell tucked the personal radio into his coat pocket and switched off the receiver. The bushes ended beside a high wire fence and both men had to crawl on their bellies along the fence line towards the rear of the building. The high wall ended at the wire fence and it was clear to both men that they had overlooked the possibility of a vehicle being parked in the premises next door early on in the evening. The villains would then, only have to arrive on foot at a later hour, cut the fence and climb through. No one would see them and they had a good chance of getting away with it. It became all too clear to Bell now. He halted Peterson and outlined what he had thought.

"We'll be better off getting through this fence ourselves and having a nose around the next building whilst they're in the warehouse. See if we can locate a vehicle".

"Right", said Peterson, lifting the bottom wire support. "We can get under here".

Both men struggled under the fence with some difficulty. Once on the other side, they made their way across the grassy waste towards the rear of a foundry. They reached the shadows and skirted the building. They kept together and quickly surveyed the area. Slowly they made their way back to the end of the foundry nearest to the warehouse fence. The space between the two buildings was in utter darkness. The building was irregular in shape and Bell slipped along the end wall until he reached a large recess where the building formed a small courtyard.

He glanced around the corner and to his delight, made out the darker shape of a box van. His pulse quickened. No matter how many times he had been on these jobs, how often he had cornered suspects or come across someone screwing a building, the effect upon his pulse rate was always the same.

He dashed back to the end of the building where Peterson waited.

"It's there", he said. "The van is just around that corner, in a courtyard. It's well hidden from the road and if they've cut the fence just opposite they'll have a clear run. We've bloody got 'em Bill". He grinned widely.

"Good", said Peterson rubbing his hands together, excited at the prospect. "What do we do now?"

"Get back to the end of the foundry out of earshot and radio back to the station. I want both ends of the road covered. Tell them to instruct the drivers not to use headlights or blue lights. Just to arrive nice and easy like and wait each end of the road until I give the word, then they can close in. They'll be trapped".

"Okay", Peterson replied, and he disappeared with the radio.

Bell kept watch on the fence, waiting for any indication that the thieves were coming back. He realised that to make the job worth while, the thieves would have to make several trips back and forth in order to get sufficient gear to fill the van.

There was a movement the other side of the fence. Bell saw nothing, just heard the sound of feet hitting the concrete pathway at the rear of the warehouse, a mumbling noise, and a scrapping sound followed by a second pair of feet dropping onto concrete. Bell crouched low and peered carefully around the corner. The fence moved and trembled slightly and then a carton was pushed through, followed by the figure of a man. A second box followed and a second man appeared. They lifted the boxes and hurried across the dark space towards the spot where the van was parked. A noise behind him told Bell that Peterson had rejoined him.

"Ssshh, they're at the van", Bell whispered. "Keep down and keep quiet".

They knelt on the grassy ground and said nothing. A scuffling noise heralded the return sprint of the two intruders, and Bell saw them disappear through the wire fence again.

"Good", he said. "They've gone back for some more".

Bell and Peterson watched and waited as the two men worked feverishly for some thirty minutes, backwards and forwards from the warehouse to the van. After the sixth trip, Bell estimated that the van would be almost full. The cartons, approximately two feet square, would just about be filling up the space in the van.

"I reckon this will be the last trip", he said to Peterson, still kneeling behind him. "Give me the radio".

Peterson handed him the radio and changed positions.

"Now listen", Bell said. "As soon as we hear the van start up, I'll radio to tell the cars to move in. They should get the van just as it drives out on to the road. We'll move out behind it and we'll have to run, okay?".

"Right", confirmed Peterson.

The fence vibrated again and the familiar struggle with the cartons was repeated. Two figures slipped across the dark area and the thump thump of the cartons being loaded was this time followed by the hollow sound of the metal doors being closed.

"Now", breathed Bell.

The van's front doors clunked as they were closed gently, and the engine whined as it was coaxed into life.

"Move in now", said Bell over the radio. "Van's just moving out of the premises. Two men aboard".

The van rolled forward and turned right towards the road. Lights were not yet switched on. It reached the road and accelerated, turning right again and the lights came on at the same time.

Bell and Peterson started running in order to get a chance of catching up with the van as soon as the patrol cars stopped it. As they reached the road, Bell saw two cars approaching from one end of the road. They were being driven abreast, taking up the entire width of the narrow road. A similar pattern from the opposite direction, completely sealed the road. The two Detectives sprinted towards the van, now slowing down, hesitating. It was obvious that the diver didn't know quite what to do.

The van stopped and the patrol cars spilled men from both sides, surrounding the van. Bell and Peterson puffed and panted as they arrived and stood leaning against the doors of the van. They were unable to speak at first.

"Great job", Bell puffed at last, acknowledging the efficiency of the uniformed Officers. "Beautiful timing".

The two men in the van sat motionless, unbelieving. "Alright you two", said Bell. "You're both under arrest for warehouse-breaking". He opened the driver's door. "Get out". He reached for the handcuffs tucked into his waistband. "I suppose I'd better tell you that you don't have to say anything but if you do, it'll go in evidence". He didn't believe in the fancied up version of the caution. Didn't really believe in it at all for all the good it did. Still, it had to be said so he said it in the best manner he found applicable in the circumstances.

"Yeah, I know all that jazz", said the long-haired man, jumping down from the cab.

"Good", said Bell, snapping on the cuffs and handing the man to the uniformed Sergeant standing nearby.

"Can you take this one in for us please, Serge?", he said. "My car is right over the back".

Peterson went through a similar procedure on the nearside as he arrested the second man.

"Who bleedin' grassed?", said the second man as Peterson pushed him towards the uniformed Officer by the van. "some bastard obviously set us up".

"Wouldn't you like to know?" said Bell, smiling now for the first time in many hours.

A uniformed Constable jumped behind the wheel of the van and drove the vehicle away to the Police station. Bell remained with the Sergeant for a few minutes whilst Peterson sprinted across the car park to pick up the car from the bushes.

"Nice job", said the Sergeant. "How did it come off then?".

"Tip off", said Bell, not wishing to disclose too much, "paid off for a change".

"Good for you there was a cooperative uniform shift on duty tonight", the Sergeant said, grinning.

There was always some friendly rivalry between the two departments. Some took pleasure in running down the other branches, unjustifiably so, but then, there were always people like that. Others did it as a matter of course. However, when it came to the crunch, both departments could be relied upon to work in close cooperation to achieve a common end. Tonight, success was due almost entirely to the efficiency of the uniformed department interpreting the instructions of their Detective colleagues.

Half an hour later, back at the station, Bell took off his jacket and loosened his tie. He sipped a cup of steaming coffee and shuffled an armful of files, each relating to different warehouse-breaks. Bell knew that the night ahead would be a long one. He prepared himself for a long, tedious session of comparing notes, interrogations and form filling. At least he had the two men stone-cold on the current job and there was nothing they could do or say to get themselves out of that one. Half the battle was over and, with any luck, they would cough the other jobs too.

By nine o'clock the following morning, Bell was thoroughly exhausted. Peterson had gone off at six, all the preliminaries having been competed. Bell was feeling pleased with his night's work. The two villains had been caught on the job. Four thousand pounds worth of property had been recovered at the time and the men had admitted being implicated in all the other recorded crimes involving warehouses over the past few months. They had even given names of the people who had received the goods and it would only be a matter of time before they too, would be arrested. With any luck, more of the gear would be recovered.

Chief Inspector Frost came into the office at his normal brisk pace.

"Morning all", he said as he hurried through the main office, towards his own. He glanced around the room, saw Bell sitting at his desk, and stopped dead.

"Still here Bell?", he said, surprised. "Or just back again?"

"Still here Sir", said Bell, stifling a yawn.

"Well how did it go last night then?", Frost asked, not expecting a positive reply.

"Got 'em both on the job Sir", replied Bell. "Four thousand quid's worth of property too".

"Good Lord, are they inside now?", Frost asked.

"Both down the cells Sir", Bell answered. "They have admitted all the other jobs too Sir", he said, "and I'm just about bushed".

The Chief Inspector was impressed. He knew that he could trust Bell to do a good job, but he didn't expect such a thorough and satisfactory end to this one.

"Well done, Harry", he said. It was indeed a compliment, for Frost was rarely heard to address any of his men by their Christian names.

"I've finished my statement and report now Sir. There will be a number of houses and shops to be searched later on and some more bodies to lift. I don't feel able to keep on going much longer though, do you think someone else can carry on from here?"

Frost looked at Bell. "God, he looks tired", he thought. "Certainly Harry", he said. Take the rest of today off. Have a good rest. You're day off tomorrow anyway, so we'll see you on Friday".

Bell handed him his report.

"I've already charged them with last night's job, Sir. I'll leave the remainder until we've decided upon the line we are going to follow".

"Fine", said Frost, "now off you go, have a good rest - and well done".

The old car trundled along the road and took them out of town to a smart new restaurant which had only been open a few weeks. Bell had visited the place a couple of times on duty and had promised that he would take Sue there for a meal one of these days.

He pulled into the spacious car par and locked up; not that anyone would have wanted to steal the car anyway. His actions were really motivated by force of habit.

He took his wife's arm and they entered the large, plush foyer, and immediately fell into the mood of the place. Several bars led off the main entrance and dinner-suited waiters dashed about, trays of drinks held high. A top-hatted doorman greeted them and wished them both a good evening.

Bell took his wife's coat, handed them to the hat check girl, and they went into the softly lit lounge with high stools placed all around a circular bar in the centre of the room. Taped music played from some discreetly placed speakers, and the customers spoke to each other in mere whispers.

"Mmmmm, this is nice", said Sue, squeezing Harry's arm. "Quite a romantic place".

"Glad you like it", said Bell, looking around at the faces of the people in the room. It was a habit he could not break, whenever he entered a bar or crowded room in a public place. The sign of the ever observant policeman.

The barman served them with cocktails and a waiter hovered in readiness to take their advanced orders for the meal, which proved to be superb., and the attention lavished upon them by zealous waiters, made the meal seem like a banquet. Sue couldn't remember when last she had enjoyed an evening out so much.

They sat in the coffee lounge after eating, and Bell ordered two brandies to follow.

"Thanks for all this, Harry", Sue said. "It really was worth waiting for". Her eyes shone and her smile was generous.

"I'm glad you enjoyed it", he replied. "I hate it when we have to give up a night out or even a night at home together, when I have to work on".

Sue held his hand tightly. "I didn't really mean what I said about you being with other women".

"I know", he sighed. He drew on his cigarette and blew smoke towards the ceiling. He became aware of a man at the bar watching them. He couldn't place the man, and wondered if he was in fact mistaken. He ignored the man, but from time to time his eyes wandered towards the stranger who was still watching them.

"Do you know that man?", Sue asked. "He's been watching us for quite some time now".

"Can't say I do", replied Bell, feeling a little annoyed at the intrusion. The man was about forty, thick-set and powerful looking with dark hair, greying about the temples. He had a tanned face, and sipped brandies. His eyes were cold and calculating.

"Ignore him", whispered Bell. "He'll probably go away".

They finished their brandies and got up to go. As they walked towards the door, the man got up and followed them out.

"Won't be a second", Bell said to his wife, leaving her near the hat check girl. "Just going to the Gents".

He went into the Gentlemen's toilets and combed his hair. He ran the tap to wash his hands and sure enough, the door opened and the man from the bar cam in and looked around. Just the two of them occupied the room.

"Harry Bell, I believe", the man said softly.

"Who are you?", said Bell, surprised that the man knew his name.

"I am William Chandler", the man said.

"I don't know you or your name", said Bell.

"Oh, but you will", Chandler replied. "You will be hearing my name a lot in the future".

"So who, or should I say what, are you?", Bell spat, anxious to find out what it was all about.

"Last night you dealt very efficiently with some acquaintances of mine. Not close friends mind you, but nevertheless, acquaintances. I admire the way you work Bell. You see, I've heard about you before. You have cost me considerable amounts of money from time to time, although I don't suppose you realise it. However, I won't beat about the bush. I have no doubt that it is too late to stop the wheels of your latest detection from going fully into motion, but I would like to make you a proposition".

Bell was cautious. He smelt a 'frame up', and wondered how much this man was about to offer him. He looked swiftly towards the cubicles in the room as if to confirm that there were no 'rubber-heeled' Officers waiting to hear him accept a bribe.

"Just what are you offering me?", Bell snapped. "I'm not bloody bent and you know it".

"Good heavens", replied the man. "I'm not suggesting that you are. All I am going to offer you is a square and fair deal. I certainly do not intend to offer you a bribe".

"What sort of a deal?", Bell said.

"Well now", Chandler drawled. "I've been watching you and your wife. I find her most attractive and it occurs to me that you are very fond of her. Wouldn't it be a pity if she was to meet with a nasty accident some time?"

"You bastard", roared Bell, raising his fist as if to strike the man. Chandler cut him short.

"Don't try it, Mr. Bell", he threatened. "It would do you no good at all". His voice was like a razor's edge.

"Alright", said Bell. "Just what is it I have got to do?"

"That's better", said Chandler. "Now just listen and listen well. I have got a lot of interests in this town and a lot of money is tied up in those interests. Now, I know that you have your job to do, but let me say this much - certain jobs fall within your province. I know from past experience, that most jobs to do with warehouse-breaks, fall to you. Those jobs interest me, and I have lost a lot of money on them, especially after your operation last night. I do not intend to lose a lot more money, and my proposition is just this. In the event of future warehouse jobs being pulled off in this town, I want your full cooperation. I want to be informed of any Police operations or planned raids in the same connection. In short, Mr. Bell - you will keep me informed. In return, your wife will keep her good looks. Do I make myself clear?"

Bell leaned heavily against the wall. What could he do? What could he say?

"I.....don't believe it", he said, his voice a mere whisper. "I just don't believe it".

"You'd better believe it, Bell", said Chandler. "You'd better believe it". He opened the door and disappeared into the night.

Bell rejoined his wife. He felt as if he had been beaten thoroughly. He was shaking and his face had drained.

"Whatever is the matter?", Susan asked. "You look ill darling".

"Yes", said Bell. "I don't feel so good".

"You poor darling", Sue whispered. "Come on, you've had too much for one day".

All the way home, Bell thought about what Chandler had said. "Christ", he mused, "Things just don't happen like this".

"What's that dear?", his wife said.

"Oh....nothing", he replied.

Bell slept fitfully that night, and got up three times to smoke. Sue slept soundly however, and didn't even awake when her husband got up. Bell paced about downstairs, trying to think of a way out. Who this man was, he didn't know. He had never heard the name Chandler before, and certainly did not recognise the man's face.

At eight o'clock Sue awoke and found her husband had already dressed. He was in the kitchen drinking coffee.

"Good morning darling", she said, "are you alright this morning?"

"Fine", he said. "Look Sue, I've got to just pop down the nick for a while. Won't be long though, okay".

"What have you got to go there for?", she asked cautiously.

"Just something I want to check on, nothing much, but important enough".

Susan looked at him and shook her head. "Oh alright then", she said at last. "I didn't think we'd get the two whole days together without the job interfering".

"Won't be long", he said, and dashed out of the door.

He searched every record in the station. He telephoned headquarters and all the intelligence units, but could find nothing on the man Chandler. He toyed with the idea of reporting the threat to the Chief Inspector, but had second thoughts. If Chandler found out that he had crossed him, then there might just be repercussions. He must prevent that at all costs.

He drove home again at a leisurely pace. He spent the day in the garden doing nothing in particular. Sue loved having him about her at home all day, and stopped working several times to embrace him. Bell felt impatient. He wanted something constructive to happen so that he could trap Chandler into making a wrong move. He wanted that man and he intended to fix him up somehow - but how?, that was the problem.

Next day, Bell arrived at the Office bright and early. He was eager now to get to work. Four more people had been arrested and charged in connection with the warehouse jobs and other arrests were expected soon. He studied the files and the Chief Inspector briefed him as to his next moves.

"It appears", said Front, "that someone is financing these small shopkeepers in order that they can buy the stuff from the villains. It works something like this. A Mr. Big, we'll call him, picks a radio and television shop where business is not too good. He approaches the shop owner and makes him a proposition. He offers to lend the shop owner sufficient money to enable him to buy a load of stolen gear from which he will be able to make a handsome profit. The shop owner accepts the proposition on terms that he will repay the loan at a minute rate of interest".

Bell frowned. "But how does that pay off?"

"Ah!", said Frost. "That's where the crunch comes. Once the man has accepted the loan, Mr. Big arranges for a front man to call and offer a load of stolen gear. The shop owner accepts and hands over the money which apparently goes back to Mr. Big, who, incidentally, I believe, engineers the theft in the first place. Finally, having implicated the shop owner in the dishonest handling of the property, he blackmails the man into handing over twenty percent of his total takings in return for silence".

Bell whistled softly. "What a miserable racket - the bastard".

"Well", went on Frost, "multiply that by about a hundred small shop owners, all conned by the same Mr. Big, and we have a considerable amount of profit being made by that man, plus a lot of misery for the unfortunate shop owners".

"I can see that", said Bell. "Does anyone know who this Mr. Big is?"

"That's just the point", said Frost. "No one has actually met him in person. He has always made his first approach by telephone and thereafter a runner has made all the arrangements and connections".

"Crafty bastards".

"What's that?", said Frost.

"Nothing Sir". Bell rubbed his chin. "And I take it then, that the people you've roped in are shop owners", he went on.

"Correct", replied Frost. "Just the small fry".

"And now we want Mr. Big himself, together with his front men".

"That's right Bell, and that will be your sole assignment from now on".

"Christ Almighty", whistled Bell, realising the job ahead of him.

"He won't help you Bell", said Frost, icily. "You'll have to get your informants to work".

"Yes sir", said Bell.

He left and went to his desk where he made up his diary.

"Where the hell do I go from here?", he asked himself. "If Mr. Big is who I think he is, then I'm in for a tough time. How the hell do I crack him and keep Sue out of trouble at the same time?"

He spent a long time pondering over Sue's predicament. He didn't want to tell our outright, that she was in danger. On the other hand, he couldn't just do nothing and risk getting her beaten up or perhaps even worse. "A holiday", he thought. "That's it, I must send her away. But for how long? She won't just go off without a good reason and anyway, we've never had separate holidays since we've been married....she just won't wear it". He thought about it some more.

"Well, Bell, are you just going to sit there all day, or are you going to get out and do something about that job?", Frost barked.

"Right away Sir", said Bell, cursing the man under his breath. "Bloody good kid, shouting the odds from his bloody office. Bet he couldn't find a bloody bag of straw in a stable". He got up and put on his raincoat. He slipped out and didn't take a car. He walked down town and went to a dirty old newspaper vendor's stall.

"Anything for me today Charlie old friend?", he said.

"Sorry Guv", the weathered Charlie sniffed. "I ain't 'eard nuffink".

"What nothing at all?", said Bell, sounding disappointed. "What about warehouses?".

"No Sir, Mr. Bell", Charlie said. "Not today".

"Okay Charlie". Bell put his hand in his pocket and took out a handful of money. "Here, buy yourself an ounce of baccy". He dropped the money on the bench top. "See you later perhaps".

"Thank you Guv. I'll see what I can ferret out".

Bell walked on through the Friday morning crowds. The shops were busy and the traffic heavy. He coughed as he took in a lung full of diesel fumes from a passing lorry. He caught sight of a young man on the other side of the road; rough looking fellow with an uncombed mop of hair, and an old leather jacket. Ricky James was one of the local Yobbos whom Bell had locked up one night for damaging a bus shelter. He hadn't had any choice on that occasion, but to bring them in. He had been out with a young probationer attached to C.I.D. for a couple of weeks and it wouldn't have done to ignore an obvious crime in a probationer's presence. Besides, it would have given the fellow the wrong impression. So he had lifted the lot of them and charged them with wilful damage. Since then, James had come to him from time to time with little bits of information. He felt obliged to bring such quips of interest to Bell, since there were a couple of matters still not yet settled. Bell was considering whether or not to file charges of theft of bottles of milk against James, from some months back. He had seen the lad pinch the milk off a doorstep, and had nabbed him. He figured that it would be wise to 'keep this one on the books', just boiling over, in case of the need at a later date. It was this knowledge, and the fear of new charges being brought whilst he was on probation, that encouraged James to bring information to Bell.

Bell crossed the road and followed James up the hill towards the White Cow cafe, a regular haunt of the local Yobs. James ambled along the road, kicking a Coca Cola tin in the gutter. He crossed the road and went into the cafe. Bell watched from the other side of the road and stood back in a shop doorway. James ordered something from the counter girl and went to play on the pin ball machine. He had his back to the door. The place was almost empty.

Bell stepped into the cafe quietly, and nodded to the girl to indicate that he wanted nothing. He went up behind James. Loud music was playing from a juke box in the corner.

"Got anything for me today then, Ricky?", he said in a not too friendly tone. It didn't do to be too nice to these yobs. James swung round, taken unawares.

"Blimey, Mr. Bell - you crept up on me. Gave me quite a turn, you did".

"Did I now?", said Bell, keeping his face straight and menacing. "What you doing with yourself then? No work?"

"No, I got the sack, didn't I?"

"What for - bloody pinching?"

"Please Mr. Bell - you know I wouldn't knock off the firm's gear", he said smiling.

"Not bleeding much", said Bell. "So what you going to do about another job then?"

"Dunno. I'll have to see what the labour's got for me this morning".

"Yeah. Well, what have you got to tell me?", asked Bell. "You haven't been to see me lately".

"Well, you know how it is Mr. Bell", said James, trying it on. "Fings don't come too easy these days".

"Don't they? Well I know something that's coming real easy for you if you don't hurry up and start working for me. You know, that milk still hasn't been officially recorded yet..." Bell raised his eyebrows. "You know what I mean now don't you?"

"Alright Mr. Bell", said James, "I'll have something for you this afternoon, you watch".

"You bet I will", said Bell. "It may be, if you don't start coming up with something worth while that I'll come up with something worth putting you on for, know what I mean, James?"

"Yes Sir, got you. You can depend on me Mr. Bell".

"Good", said Bell. "See you".

He walked out and made his way towards the town, his mind racing for inspiration. He went towards the market and wondered about radios and tape recorders. "Who would be a likely customer", he mused. He went into a secondhand shop which displayed everything from fishing tackle to old comics, radios, tape recorders, books, clothes, silver ware, and just about every kind of item littered the shelves and tables.

"Hello, Mr. Bell", greeted the kindly old man in a cloth cap. "Nice to see yer".

"Hello Piper", said Bell pleasantly. "How's trade then?"

"Well you know 'ow it is these days. Up and down so to speak. Nothin' much doin', Mr. Bell. How's yerself?"

"Oh, not too bad, Piper. Know anything?"

"Got sumfink for you, Mr. Bell", he said, looking over his shoulder and all around. He lowered his voice. "'smornin' it were. Young chap come in wiv a silver watch. I got it right 'ere. Didn't like the looks of 'im, you know. Gave 'im a quid for it". He reached over and pulled an old fob watch from under the counter and handed it to Bell. It was a good one - very old. The cover over the face was inscribed, 'Colonel Braggs, from the Officers of the 32nd'.

"Identifiable", said Bell. "What was this chap like?"

"Youngster", said Piper. "About seventeen. Five eight I should say, thin and had greasy hair".

"What was he wearing?"

"Ah yes - wore a green windcheater thing, and old khaki trousers. Looked like he needed a good wash too".

"Say anything?", asked Bell.

"Yes. Said his uncle give him the watch and he needed a bit of money".

"Local lad would you say?"

Piper thought a while. "Now you mention it, no", he said. "Sounded like he was from up North - Scots, I should think".

"Okay", said Bell. "I'll keep the watch for now Piper. I'll check it out. If it's okay, I'll let you have it back". He put the watch into his pocket.

"Thanks, Mr. Bell", the old man said. "God bless you".

Bell dropped a packet of cigarettes on the counter. "They're your brand aren't they?", he said, smiling.

"Thank you, Mr. Bell. You're a gentleman", Piper said, snatching up the cigarettes. He beamed at the Detective. Bell made a mental note of the time and wandered off.

He passed the time of day with one or two market porters, and bought a pair of shoes from Schulster's stall. He knew that if any of them heard anything of interest, they would tell him. No one knew anything on this occasion.

At eleven thirty, he went back to the station. He dropped the watch on his desk and telephone property index at headquarters. The watch was identified as being part of the takings from a country manor house just over the County boundary, the day before. Burglary. There were no suspects.

"Well", thought Bell, "there's a suspect now, and it looks like he's on our patch".

He telephoned the headquarters of the next County and told them about the youth who had sold the watch to Piper. Then he passed the description to all the local patrols, just in case the chap was still skulking about. There was a telephone message for him to ring a number at midday. The message did not say who the caller was.

There was nothing else, so he disappeared again, and went back into the town. He had a beer in the Locomotive pub, and stood leaning against the bar, chatting to the barmaid.

"Big job the other night then?", the girl said.

"Oh?", said Bell, non-committally.

"Warehouse job, radios and what not", the girl said. "It was all in the papers today".

"Oh, yes", said Bell.

"I could do with some cheap gear myself", the girl said. "Always wanted my own stereo equipment".

"Well, you'd better ask the right people then", said Bell, jokingly. "Come to think of it, you might even strike lucky. Tell you what, you find out who's flogging that kind of stuff cheap, and I'll see to it that you get a stereo set free, and on the level too".

The girl looked at him. "Okay", she said. "You're on".

"Only keep it quiet", Bell said, winking and tapping the side of his nose.

At five to twelve, he stepped out and walked towards the telephone kiosk outside the railway station. He waited until exactly twelve o'clock then dialled the number he had been given. He waited as the digits clicked over then rang out somewhere. The ringing stopped and a voice answered, giving the number only.

"Bell here".

"Ah, Mr. Bell", the voice on the line said. It was a familiar voice, though not particularly friendly.

"Chandler", said Bell, disappointed.

"Of course it is", said the voice. "Now listen to me carefully. I am going to give you a telephone number which you can ring any time you have something to tell me. It is not my home or office and no one can connect me with the number. The person to whom the number is allocated has agreed to accept calls for me at any time, and I telephone him from time to time for messages. If absolutely necessary, he can get in touch with me immediately, but no one will ever get him to disclose my identity or whereabouts. The number is 73529. Remember it Mr. Bell, and don't forget to use it". The line went dead.

Bell jotted down the number in his pocket diary and left the kiosk. He was still wondering how he was going to get this man hooked without endangering his wife. "There must be a way somehow", he thought--------"The anonymous informant", he thought on......"I wonder how much he knows, whoever he is". Then it occurred to him that the man was just hoping to get his own back on a couple of small time crooks who had done the dirty on him at some time. "That's more like it", he mused.

He went back to the station and had some lunch in the canteen. Not much of a lunch, but then, what canteen supplies anything better? After lunch, he spent the afternoon making the rounds of the cafes and milk bars, talking to the owners here and customer there. He played the pin-ball machines, and quipped double meaningly with the yobbos hanging about, out of work, yet not hard up for money. He contacted just about every informant he could recall, and put the word out that he was in the market for information about knocked off stereo and recording gear. The word soon passed around, and Bell knew that he could relax a little and that someone would come up with a lead soon.

At six o'clock, he returned to his desk and started to wade through a mountain of paperwork. He cursed the statisticians and the bright boys who designed the forms and made the demands for such a lot of duplication one way or another. He typed for an hour, then wrote for another hour, and eventually, two neat piles of paper stood in front of him on the desk. One marked 'Pending', and the other marked 'For Court'. The remainder of the paperwork was for submission to the Chief Inspector.

Bell sighed as he leaned back in his chair. He lit a cigarette and stretched his long legs under the desk. The telephone rang. A young Detective answered it.

"Is Dinger there please?", asked the voice on the end of the wire.

"Who?", said the Detective.

"Dinger - you know, Bell", said the voice, giggling some.

"You mean Mr. Bell", said the young man "Wait a minute".

He turned and addressed Bell. "Are you in, Harry?"

"Who is it?", said Bell, "didn't you ask?"

"Who is it?", the Detective asked the caller.

"Tell him Ricky James", said the voice.

"Ricky James", repeated the Detective.

"Alright", replied Bell. "I'll have a word".

He walked over to the telephone and put the receiver to his ear.

"Bell here", he said.

"'ello Mr. Bell", said the voice. "Look, I got sumfink for you, like I said", James said eagerly. "I got word that a lorry load of radios is goin' to be knocked off tonight, from the back of the Radiomart warehouses in Finch Street. It's a big green box van with white doors. The name 'Johnsons' is written on the sides. Two blokes will be picking it up about ten o'clock, okay?".

"You sure about this?", Bell said. "I wouldn't put it past you to make up something just to keep me sweet".

"'course I'm sure, Mr. Bell", James said. "I wouldn't lie to you, would I?".

"Where did you get the gen from?", Bell asked suspiciously.

"I get around, Mr. Bell. I heard these geezers in the White Cow cafe tonight. Strangers they were, but they were whispering to each other and I just sort of overheard them like".

"You'd better be right, James", Bell threatened.

"I am, Mr. Bell, believe me, it's true".

"Okay then", said Bell. "If the gen's right, I'll see you later and put things right with you". He hung up and returned to his desk thoughtfully.

Bell looked at his watch. Eight forty. He knew that he would have to follow up the lead, and needed someone to help.

"What time you off, Reg?", he said to the young Detective.

"Ten o'clock, Harry", the young man replied.

"Can you hang on and do some obbos with me? I think we might nab a couple of lorry thieves".

"Of course I can. Just let me make a phone call to my girl, and I'll be with you".

He telephoned, and Bell heard him apologising to the girl for not being able to make their date. Bell grinned cynically, and thought "He'll be doing that kind of thing a lot more in the future if he's going to make a good Detective".

"Right, Harry", said the Detective finally. "I'm ready when you are".

They took one of the cars and drove steadily across town to the Finch Street area, then stopped and got out. They walked towards the

Radio-mart warehouse and slipped along a narrow lane leading to the rear of the premises, from the next street. Sure enough, there in the middle of the car park, standing all alone, was a large box van, green with white doors, and the name 'Johnsons' painted along the sides. There was no one about.

"Right", said Bell, rubbing his hands together in anticipation. "So far, so good. We'll just have to sit and watch the exit and when they come out, we'll get uniform to pull them in and check them".

They went back to their car where they could watch the exit, about a hundred and fifty yards away. It was the only way out. Bell looked at his watch. Nine fifty. Not long to wait, if all went to plan. He yawned and stretched himself, and cursed the governor for putting him onto this job. He thought of Sue, and another dinner shrivelled up in the oven.

"Wouldn't be so bad", he thought, "if I really was knocking off some gorgeous young bird"; like Sue suspected of him sometimes. "Women!", he said aloud.

"What's that, Harry?", said his companion.

"Oh, nothing. Just thinking aloud", Bell replied.

"Looks interesting", the younger man said, nodding towards two young men who were strolling towards the entrance to the warehouse car park. Bell sat up. Two youngsters, both dressed in jeans and denim jackets, longish hair and boots, typical milk bar cowboys, entered the car park and disappeared from sight.

"This could be it", said Bell. He started the motor and let it idle as they sat and watched.

A few minutes later, the lorry appeared and came on into the road and turned right. It drove slowly towards the edge of town, and Bell followed at a safe distance. "Get onto H.Q.", he said, "and ask them to divert a car to stop the lorry somewhere up the road".

Reg picked up the handset and transmitted the request which the operator acknowledged. They heard instructions being passed to a patrol car in the vicinity. Bell just stayed a couple of hundred yards behind the lorry. It was dark but street lights allowed him to drive with just his sidelights on.

A mile further on, a patrol car appeared from a side street, and the crew got out and waved the lorry to a halt. The lorry stopped, and Bell pulled up behind it. He dashed out and ran to the cab and opened the door.

"Okay", he said. "Don't move". He reached in and grabbed the ignition keys and put them in his pocket.

"What the hell is this?", the lorry driver said.

"You're nicked", said Bell, triumphantly - "for stealing this lorry and load".

"You're bloody joking", said the driver. "This is my regular lorry and load. I park it there in the afternoon ready for the night run to Glasgow".

"Oh yes - well what are you carrying then?", Bell asked.

"Corn Flakes", said the young driver. "Bloody Corn Flakes".

"Out", ordered Bell, and as the driver stepped down, Bell ran his hands over the man - nothing.

"Open the back", Bell ordered. The man went round to the back and opened up. Cartons marked 'Corn Flakes', filled the space. Corn Flakes. He opened several from different parts of the load. All were the same - Corn Flakes.

"Balls!", cursed Bell, "the bastard has had us over".

"So what's the game then mate?", the driver asked, sarcastically. "What the hell did you expect to find in there?"

"Never mind", said Bell. "Sorry we bothered you, you can go".

"Well thanks a bloody lot", said the other as he climbed back into the cab.

Bell dispersed the patrol car with thanks, and nodded to Reg. They returned to their car and moved off in a huff. They drove in silence for some minutes.

"What d'you think happened then, Harry?", asked the younger man.

"We've been bloody had, that's what happened", said Bell. "I'll see to it that that bastard doesn't get away with this".

He drove back to the Police Station in silence, and dropped off his colleague.

"I'm going to take the car down town, I've got some business to see to", said Bell, slipping into gear and easing away from the kerb. "See you".

A few minutes later, Bell walked into the White Cow cafe. The place was crowded with leather jacketed youngsters - stud-spangled jackets with the variety of names and designs shouting out from the background of leather, and chains hanging in confusion from the backs and arms. Long hair was the order of the place, and the constant movement of each youngster's jaws as he or she chewed gum, gave them the appearance of machines powered by perpetual motion.

Bell stood inside the door and scanned the faces for the one he was looking for. He could not see Ricky James at first. He pushed his way through the crowd. "Hey man, what's your scene?", said a long haired dirty looking lout, leaning on the counter, studying Bell. "Like a, you don't dig this joint; who you looking for, Daddyoh?"

"Get stuffed", retorted Bell, stepping on the outstretched foot and making the youngster yell.

"Watch it, Bimbo", whispered the youth's side-kick, "he's the Fuzz".

Bell made for the pinball machines and, sure enough, there was James, squatting at a table, watching the scores tick up as a cowboy pushed the buttons, tapping his plimsolled feet in time with the music from the juke box. James didn't see Bell as first, and just stared at the pin table. Then, as if telepathy had warned him, he suddenly turned and looked Bell straight in the eye. He jumped and stood up. "Why, Mr. Bell", he spluttered.

Harry Bell reached out and twisted his fingers into the front of the imitation leather jacket. He pulled James towards him and pushed his face up close to the youngster.

"Outside - now!"

"What for, Mr. Bell?", whined James.

"'cos I said so", hissed Bell. "On the double".

He released the lad and walked back towards the door. The long haired, long legged, big mouth yob was still leaning against the counter, feet still outstretched as Bell walked towards the front of the premises. In the crowd, Bell had no alternative but to stop and wait for the removal of the obstructive legs and feet. They remained where they were. The lout just looked at Bell and chewed on his gum, grinning with a mouthful of black teeth. A young girl at his side chewed slowly, pouting her lips with each movement. She grinned like her boyfriend.

"Move your big feet", growled Bell.

The youth turned to the girl and his friends at his side.

"Did anyone hear sumfink?", he said, and his mates laughed.

"I said move!", repeated Bell, deliberately omitting any pleasantries.

"There it goes again", laughed the girl who couldn't have been more than fifteen.

The greasy looking lout looked at Bell and continued grinning. "Like man, when you want Bimbo to move, you - kind of ask nice like - know what I mean...like - please. Now ask me again, fuzzy wuzzy".

There was a roar of laughter from his companions. Bell didn't hesitate. He knew that these people had to be treated like the animals they portrayed, and he knew too, that to hesitate would be to play into their hands. He drew back his right foot and swung it heavily forward, hooking his toe under the young man's ankle, lifting it off the floor. The legs shot out straight and the lout fell like a bomb onto his backside. Bell walked over the outstretched legs and made towards the door, unhurried. The place fell silent, but Bell didn't hang around. He had made his point and the lout had lost face in front of his friends. The purpose had been served.

Bell waited in the alleyway outside the White Cow cafe, and James followed him out. He sidled up to the Detective and dug his hands into his jeans pockets. Bell didn't waste time on preliminaries. He grabbed James by the lapels and lifted him bodily off his feet, crashing him against the wall.

"Right then, you slob", he began. "What about tonight then?". James was terrified.

"What d'you mean, Mr. Bell?", he whined.

"What do I mean?", yelled Bell. "I mean that bloody duff tip off you gave me. Who put you up to it, eh?"

"I heard 'em talking, that's all. Just 'eard 'em talking".

"How much did they pay you to tip me off?"

"Nuffink - honest".

"Come on, James. I'll stitch you up for a good one if you don't stop lying to me, now, who put you up to it tonight?"

"honest, Mr. Bell, I 'heard these two geezers talking in there. I don't know anyfink else. I 'eard 'em talking about knocking off this lorry load of radio gear. One of 'em was telling the other all about the job. I knew you'd like to know, so I tinkled you".

Bell released the frightened youngster and sighed.

"You'd better be on the level, James", he said.

Bell thought the matter over for a while. It had been a set-up, that was for sure. Someone had wanted the information to get back to him, but why? Then it occurred to him that whoever wanted him to believe that the lorry was being stolen with radio gear aboard, could only have wanted him to know for one reason - they wanted to see if he acted on the information. Chandler must be behind it and was testing Bell in order to see if he would do as instructed, or ignore the man's warnings and take police action regardless.

"Christ", said Bell, at last realising the implications of what had taken place.

"If Chandler was behind this hoax", he thought, "Sue could be in danger right now".

"I'll see you later", he said to James, now trembling in his plimsolls. Bell sprinted along the alley towards his car, jumped in and turned the key. The engine barked and he let out the clutch and with a screech of tyres, the car leaped forward. He drove furiously through the night traffic and sped towards the outskirts of town. His mind raced as he thought of what could be happening at his home. He jumped a set of red traffic lights and an old van pulled suddenly to a halt in the middle of the crossroads, horn blaring in protest. Bell drove on, sweat beginning to form on his brow and hands.

Chapter 4

Susan Bell stepped out of the bath and wrapped herself in a warm towelling robe. She slipped her delicate feet into a pair of lambs wool mules, and hummed a happy tune to herself as she brushed her hair. She moved about the house doing odd little chores as she waited for word of her husband.

A knock at the door brought a smile to her face.

"He must have forgotten his key", she thought as she walked towards the front door. The knocker banged again. "Alright, I'm coming", she called. She opened the door and fell backwards as the two men pushed their way in. One grabbed her by the shoulders and the other pushed her backwards into the hall. He closed the door behind him.

"In there", he ordered, and Sue tried to scream, but the first man put his big hand across her mouth. They struggled to the living room and the first man turned the television up high. The man holding her, let her go and she glared at them both, a little frightened, and wondering what it was all about.

"Who are you?", she demanded, "and what are you doing here?"

"Never mind who we are", said the first one. "The point is, we're here because that stupid husband of yours can't do as he is told. So we've come to teach him the first lesson".

"Get out!", Susan shouted. "Get out at once".

The first man, a smooth looking merchant in a grey well cut suit, and sporting a drooping moustache, lifted his hand and slapped her hard across the face, sending her sprawling onto the settee. He picked her up and slapped her again.

"We could do her a big favour, I reckon, Charlie", he said, looking at Sue.

She realised that she was only wearing a robe, and that was somewhat disarranged now. Both men were ogling her and she drew her robe across herself as if in protection of her virtue.

"That would teach him good", said the second man slowly, a wry grin spreading across his face.

"Don't you touch me", Sue sobbed.

"Take it off", ordered the first man, softly. He grinned sickeningly.

"I will not", defied Sue.

"Off!", he said again, and he made a move towards her.

The front door burst open, and Bell came crashing in. He was breathless and white faced. He saw the situation and rushed straight at the man in the grey suit. The other man made off towards the back door. Bell dived across the back of the settee and caught the suited man around the neck. He held on to him in a vice-like grip. He heard the back door slam as the second man made good his escape.

Bell struggled on the floor with the smooth looking character, and exchanged blows. He felt the man's knee dig sharply into his crutch and he winced. Bell jerked the man's head backwards on to the floor and ploughed his fist squarely into the soft face. The man lay still and silent. Bell reached for his handcuffs from his belt, and with a snip, secured the man's hands behind him.

"Oh, Harry", Sue cried burying her head into his shoulder. "It was awful".

"It's alright now", soothed Harry, "don't worry any more".

"But...how did you know?", Sue said, looking at her husband. "How did you know that they were here?"

"I didn't. It was just a guess". Bell smoothed her hair and pulled her head against his chest.

"They said it was to teach you a lesson for not doing what you were told", she sobbed. "What did they mean Harry?"

"It doesn't matter just now", he said. "I'll tell you one day. Right now, we've got to make some arrangements".

He sat her down and then walked to the telephone in the hall. He dialled.

"Hello, Sergeant Jones? Harry Bell here, Serge. I've just caught a fellow in my house attacking my wife. I've knocked him off. Can you send a crew around to take him into the nick? Thanks". He replaced the receiver and returned to Sue.

"I want you to pack a suitcase, and I'm taking you to your mother on the coast", he said. "You are going to have a holiday, whether you like it or not".

"But Harry", she protested, sitting up straight.

"No arguing, Sue", he said. "You are going. Now get something packed".

An hour later, Bell was driving South, making for the coast where his wife would be safe. He kept a constant watch on the traffic in his rear view mirror. Nothing followed him. It was a long and rather silent journey during which Sue slept fitfully from time to time. The road was clear and the night was dry with a soft moon illuminating the countryside as they drove on.

Three hours later, Bell pulled up outside the cottage on the cliffs. He helped his wife out of the car and they walked up the little path towards the door. A light shone from the living room. The door opened and Sue's mother came out to greet them. A concerned expression on her face asked the question but she said nothing until Sue volunteered the information. They embraced and went inside whilst Bell unloaded the car and followed them in. He felt tired and would have loved to stay the night, but things were pressing him and he knew that he would have to return straight away.

After a cup of coffee and a sandwich, Bell said his goodbyes and left. He warned his wife not to return home until he told her it was safe. She knew the whole story now; she insisted on being told on the way down.

"Be careful darling", she whispered as she kissed him; "ring me soon".

Bell drove steadily back to town and arrive home at seven in the morning. He was almost dead on his feet. He opened the door and there was a note telling him to contact Chief Inspector Frost as soon as he came in. He dialled the number and spoke to Frost himself. He was surprised to find Frost at the office so early.

"What's going on, Bell?", the Chief demanded. "What the hell are you playing at?"

"I can't explain it all on the phone Sir", Bell said. "I'll come to the office and explain everything. Be there in half an hour".

"Right then", said Frost. "But you'd better have a good story for me".

"Yes Sir", said Bell, drowsily. He heard the phone go dead. "Miserable bastard".

He stumbled through into the bathroom and filled the hand basin with cold water. He threw his jacket and shirt on to the chair and splashed water over his tired face and body, then rubbed down with a rough towel, trying to restore life into his tired mind. He rubbed a hand over his coarse chin, and decided to shave.

At quarter to eight, Bell, looking only slightly refreshed, ambled into the C.I.D. office at the main Police Station. He went straight to the Chief Inspector's door and knocked.

"Enter", barked Frost from inside, and Bell opened the door and strode in.

"Ah! Bell", said Frost, looking up. "Come in and sit down. Now then, what's all this about? We've had a prisoner in the cells all night without being charged. What is happening about that?; and what do you think you're doing, clearing off in the middle of a job like you did, where have you been?"

Bell told him as best as he could, of the events leading up to last night's escapade - of Chandler and his threats, and of his bogus job which had turned out to be a set-up with the lorry. He told Frost of this decision to get his wife away whilst he dug his heels in and tried to break this outfit and Chandler with it. Frost listened with interest and in silence.

"Why didn't you tell me of these threats in the first place?", Frost asked at last.

"You know how it is Sir", said Bell. "One doesn't take every threat seriously in this job. If we did, we'd always be looking over our shoulders".

"Yes, I suppose you're right. Very well, we'll have to make an all out effort to get them put away. He outlined his plan to assign additional men to the job, and then he realised that he was talking to himself.

"Bell!", he said, "are you listening to me?". There was no response. Bell was sleeping soundly in the chair.

"Bell!", Frost shouted, "wake up man".

Bell stirred, then sat upright suddenly. "Oh, sorry Sir", he muttered.

"When did you last sleep?", Frost asked.

"Well, I've been on the job since eight o'clock yesterday morning Sir", the man replied.

"Alright then", said Frost. "Get down to the charge room and charge that man, then home to bed. I'll see you again tomorrow morning".

"Thank you Sir", said Bell, standing unsteadily.

He left the room and made his way to the charge room where he saw the Duty Sergeant. The man was produced and Bell looked at him with contempt.

"Colin Broadman", he said. "You are charged, that you, on......." and finished the charge with the official caution.

"I have nothing to say", said Broadman.

"Good", replied Bell. "That makes it easier to remember in Court".

The Sergeant locked the man up again, and Bell went home to bed.

Chapter 5

Bell slept for the rest of the day. He dreamed about Sue and Chandler and the two hoodlums who had broken into his house and attacked his wife. He tossed and turned and his sleep was disturbed by the uneasiness of his mind. However, he did not wake until eight o'clock that evening.

It was dark and the house was silent. Bell sat up with a start, unable to understand why he was in bed at all at such a time. Then he remembered that his wife was away and he swung his legs over the side of the bed and got out. He stumbled towards the bathroom and ran a hot shower.

At ten o'clock, Bell walked into the Locomotive public house, and the barmaid greeted him with a pint of bitter, freshly pulled.

"Hello, Harry", she said. "Still at it, or are you off duty now?"

"Off, for the moment", Bell said, sliding onto the high stool at the bar. "Cheers", he said, taking the pint mug from her and dropping a note on the counter.

"Any news for me then?", he asked, casually.

"Nothing", the girl replied. "Can't get a line on those radios and things, no one seems to want to know".

"Well, don't push it too hard", said Bell.

He finished his drink and said goodnight. He opened the swing doors and let himself out into the cool night. The street was murky and full of shadows. This was the lower end of town and far from select. He walked along the street, passing doorways occupied by couples copulating or just necking. A gang of louts hung about near the coffee bar, one sitting on top of a parking meter, swinging his legs across the pavement. Bell walked past them and heard one make a remark about the Fuzz. He ignored the remark and noted the youth's face mentally for future reference. "His day will come", Bell thought, sagely.

Bell didn't know quite what he wanted to do with himself. He felt he should be at the station or out looking for villains. He had nothing to go home for now that Sue was away, and he felt guilty about just hanging around.

He walked past a dark alleyway which led to the rear of the big departmental store in the High Street. A scuffling sound in the darkness brought him to a halt. He stood in the shadows just inside the alley and listened. He could see nothing. The scuffling sound became more prominent and he heard an occasional grunt, then a cry as if for help. Bell wasted no more time. He sprinted down the alleyway towards the sounds, and then heard footsteps disappearing towards the far end. He caught a glimpse of a leather jacketed youth scaling the wall, chains and studs adorning the old leather motor cycling jacket. The figure disappeared and Bell stopped.

A groan, just a few feet away, made Bell turn and flick on his cigarette lighter. There, on the ground, he saw an old tramp, slumped against a dustbin. He was bleeding from a bad gash on his face and his head was becoming a darker red with each second. Bell knelt beside the poor man and reassured him. He examined the injury on the head and saw a terrible gash some four inches long.

"What happened?", asked Bell. "Did you get a good look at him?"

"Dunno", breathed the old man. "Just jumped me like. I was lookin' for a place to doss down for the night. Just got 'ere and 'e jumped me. 'it me wiv summink and went through me pockets. 'as 'e got me watch?"

"Where do you keep it?", Bell said.

"In me pocket, 'ere", the old man replied, reaching for his waistcoat pocket. "It's gone", he said at last.

"What's it look like?", Bell queried.

"Gold fob watch, wiv a cover on the front. 'as me dad's name on it. George Tucker, on the inside. 'ad it twenty-five years, I 'ave".

"Alright", said Bell. "Come on then old mate, let's get you off to the hospital, you need some treatment".

He lifted the old man to his feet and they staggered towards the street. Bell helped Tucker to the telephone kiosk and dialled treble nine to summon the ambulance. He then telephoned the station and put out a message for attention to the youth he had seen going over the wall.

The ambulance arrived within a few minutes, and Bell outlined the position to the attendant and put the old man inside. The ambulance drove off and Bell knew how he was going to spend the rest of the evening.

Chapter 6

The White Cow cafe was still noisy and full of smoke. As Bell opened the door, the music blared out from the juke box, and he winced as the noise penetrated his ears. Leather jacketed yobs leaned against the counter as usual, and crowded the pin tables. The same old crowd doing the same old things, chewing the same stale gum and showing off to each other. A handful of girls wearing the same kind of leather jacket uniforms as the boys, sprawled across the tables and Bell could smell the acrid and unmistakeable odour of cannabis; but in such a crowd, it would be stupid to even try to discover exactly who was smoking the stuff.

Bell stood inside the door, hands deep in his coat pocket, collar turned up. He glared at the yobs by the counter. Someone started to sing an oldie pop song - "Fuzzy Wuzzy wuzn't Fuzzy, wuz he", and laughter trickled through the crowd.

Bimbo Parks chewed on his gum, a sneer on his ugly face; one hand in his jacket pocket. His left hand was swinging a gold chain attached to something in the pocket. He faced Bell defiantly and raised his bushy eyebrows. He turned round and walked towards the pin ball tables, and Bell saw the chains swinging on the back of his jacket and the word 'Bimbo' worked in brass studs across the back.

Bell had seen enough and his guess had proved correct. He followed Bimbo across the crowded floor, pushing bodies aside as he went. He grabbed the leather-clad shoulder and swung the youth around to face him. Bimbo glared and shrugged the hand away.

"Git your bleedin' 'ands off me, copper", he hissed; his mouth was working in all shapes and patterns as he chewed his gum.

"You're nicked", said Bell, calmly,

"Whaddya mean, I'm nicked", said Bimbo Parks. "What for?"

"I am arresting you for robbery", said Bell, snatching the gold chain from the hands of the youth. He yanked the chain and the gold fob watch came out of the top pocket. Bell tucked it into his own pocket and reached for the handcuffs which he always carried. He went to snap them on to the youth's wrists when another two of the leather jacket brigade moved towards him, threateningly.

"Let 'im go", one of them said, "or I'll bloody bust yer 'ead open". He picked up a heavy glass sugar pourer from the table.

Bell looked at the two and tightened his grip on Bimbo Parks' arm. "I am a Police Officer, and this man is under arrest", he said. "Now if anyone tries to stop me, I'll take whatever action I find necessary, now get out of my way".

The first youth came on and raised the pourer as if to strike Bell. Bell waited no longer, he swung the handcuffs in a wide arc and the free bracelet struck the tall youth across the side of the face, drawing blood immediately. The remainder stood back.

"You're bloody nicked too", said Bell, and he cuffed the two youths together and pushed them towards the door.

"Anyone else fancy their chances", he said, looking around the room, "I'll settle them too". No one moved.

Bell paraded the two youths through the streets on foot, to the Central Police Station. He dragged them through the door and handed them to the Station Sergeant.

"What have we here then, Harry?", the Sergeant said.

"One for robbery with violence and this one for obstruction". He related the facts and put the two down in the cells whilst he prepared the charge sheets.

Half an hour later, Bell charged them both and locked them up for the night. He would ask the Court for a remand in custody in the morning.

He called in the night duty Detective and got him to drive to the hospital. He told the other of the events of the evening. They arrived at the hospital and went into the casualty department. A young Sister was busy stitching up a drunk who had fallen over the pavement and cut his head.

"Hello Harry", she said, looking up. "What brings you here then?"

"The old tramp", said Bell, smiling at the Sister. "He was robbed".

"Oh yes", said the Sister. "Poor old sod".

"How is he?", asked Bell.

"He'll live, but we're keeping him in for a few days. Do you want to see him?"

"Please".

"He's in the end cubicle, help yourself". She turned and the drunk winced as the thread pulled.

"Thanks", said Bell, winking, and he went to the end cubicle and pulled the curtain aside. The old man turned his head to see who had come in.

"Hello pop", said Bell. "How you feeling now then?"

"Got an 'eadache", said the old man. "Who are you?"

"I'm the fellow who found you, remember?", said Bell, holding up the gold fob watch and chain.

"Hey, that's my watch", the old man exclaimed.

"Good", said Bell. "Well you'll be glad to know I've got the bastard who did you over and nicked it".

"Don't 'ave to go to Court, do I?", the old man said with a frown. "I don't like them places".

"I'm afraid you will", replied Bell, "but it won't hurt", he said, grinning.

"'spose you want a statement or summink then, do you?" he said with a sigh.

"Yes, it won't take long", replied Bell softly, taking out a form and undoing his pen. "I'll help you with it".

"Wha d'ya reckon will 'appen to 'em then?", Tucker asked, easing himself on the hard bed.

"Dunno", said Bell, "that'll be up to the Court, but the bastard ought to go down for bloody life".

Bell took down the statement and finally said his farewell to the old tramp.

"Have a good sleep, and take advantage of the good food whilst you're in here", he said in a friendly tone, his hand resting reassuringly on the old man's shoulder.

Chapter 7

Harry Bell felt satisfied with his night's work as he drove home at three o'clock in the morning. He knew that he had got Bimbo Parks stitched up good, and that he would probably go down for a long stretch. The Yard had come up with a fair list of previous convictions against him, and that would help to put him away for a reasonable length of time.

The next morning, Harry Bell reported for duty and plunged into a pile of paperwork. Always paperwork, he never seemed to get to an end of it all. It didn't matter how much time one spent on the paper, more jobs came in, and before you knew what was happening, the paperwork had built up again. It was a never ending process and the bane of the Detective's life.

"Nice little job last night then, Harry", said Bill Peterson. "Can't keep away from it can you?"

"Well, you know how it is", replied Bell, lighting a cigarette and pulling another file from his desk. He made a few notes on the cover of the file marked 'Robbery with Violence', and more notes on the file marked 'Obstructing a Police Office'.

An hour later, Bell stood in the Court Room beside the prosecuting solicitor who made an application for a remand in custody. The Clerk to the Court put questions to Bell who gave evidence of arrest on oath, and outlined the case briefly.

"Very well, remanded in custody for seven days", said the magistrate.

The application for remand in custody for the youth charged with obstruction was refused, and Bernard Smedley walked away smirking.

Bell returned to his office and set about preparing papers for the next appearance. He cleared a fair amount of outstanding paperwork and at lunch time, made his way to the station canteen for a roast beef lunch. He ate and joked with his colleagues and listened with interest to their conversations. His fellow Officers were always interesting and one could invariably learn something from everyone. Bell never refused to listen to anyone.

Chapter 8

He didn't get his extra men to help track down Chandler and his compatriots. The sheer volume of work prevented Frost from writing off more men for the task. Bell just had to manage on his own, for the time being anyway. He settled down to clearing his plate of outstanding work so as to leave himself ready for any lead that might come up in the warehouse rackets. He was not to know that his mission would develop through other channels.

"Can you come with me to interview a girl about a shoplifting job, Harry?", Bill Peterson said, sidling up to Bell's desk. "You know how it is, I don't want to go chatting up young girls on my own, you know - allegations and all that".

"Where is it?", Bell replied, still sifting through a pile of papers.

"Bourne Hill", said Peterson. "She's a bit of a slag, and she's got pre-cons for shoplifting. She was seen lifting some foodstuffs in the supermarket, but they couldn't stop her in time. She was identified by the Store Detective".

"Is that all you're going to see her about?", queried Bell.

"Well, no. As a matter of fact, I rather fancy we'll find some gear there from that jewellers that got done a couple of days ago. Her boyfriend, what's his name, er, Jimmy Bunce - I think he was involved and I'm pretty sure she's holding the stuff for him".

"Okay", said Bell with a long sigh. "I've had enough of this bloody paperwork for today anyway. You ready to go now then?"

"Any time you are", replied Peterson.

"Right - let's go then".

They walked to the station yard and got out the old estate car which they often used for observations. It didn't look like a police car, and served a useful purpose. Peterson drove through the arched gateway, out into the narrow street and down the hill. The one way system was a damned nuisance and caused them to drive about a mile further than necessary. Ten minutes later, they cleared the traffic and turned into a quiet but dirty street behind the parkland which was nothing more than an open-air dossing ground for wino's and layabouts.

Bourne Hill was one of those streets that every big town has, full of drop outs, junkies, prostitutes and small time villains. Half of them were cohabiting with the wives of men currently serving prison sentences, and as each man was convicted and sent down, so another would take his place in stale, unclean beds.

Number twenty-five, basement apartment, was dark and smelly. The only window at the front was curtained and the steps leading down to the door, were filthy and overgrown with weeds, smelling of urine from last night's drunks. The door, a discoloured, once blue was flaking and the number twenty-five was painted in eight inch letters in white paint which had run halfway down the door.

Bell exhaled and turned his nose up at the sight of the place. He screwed his face up at the idea of having to go into such a dive.

"Christ Bill, you don't half pick the elite residences don't you, mate?", he said sarcastically.

"Wait till she offers you a cup of tea then", quipped Peterson.

"Well, as of now, I've stopped drinking tea", said Bell.

Peterson knocked the door with his key ring. There was no knocker or bell push. There was no reply. He knocked again, this time banging his foot against the rotting door. Bell ambled to the window and peered in, hoping to get a glimpse inside through a chink in the curtain. He tapped the glass with a coin - nothing.

"Come on, Bill, she ain't in", said Bell.

"No, hang about a bit", said Peterson. "I want to get this one over with and I don't want to have to come back. Half the street will have seen us already and if there's anything in there now, it'll be gone if we don't see her before they do".

There was a cough from above, and Bell looked up in time to catch an eyeful of cigarette ash. A fat, scruffy looking woman was leaning out of a sash window immediately above them, street level.

"What do you bastards want then?", she sneered.

"Come to see Penny", said Peterson. "Know where she is?"

"Nope. Ain't seen 'er today. Funny that is though, 'cos she always comes up for a cup of tea dinner times wiv me. Ain't seen 'er at all today though, come to fink of it".

"Has she gone out?"

"I dunno. Don't s'pose so. Hey, 'er milk's still on the step too. Now that's unusual, she always takes that in before dinner. Funny that".

"When did you last see her then?", asked Peterson.

"Last night, 'bout eleven o'clock. She came in on 'er own for a change. 'er boyfriend mostly stays the night wiv 'er."

The two men looked at each other. It was not that unusual to find people out at four o'clock in the afternoon. Why should they concern themselves? But there was something in the fat woman's attitude that made them both feel a little uneasy.

"Does she go to work?", asked Peterson.

The fat woman laughed and blew more ash from the cigarette which was stuck to her lower lip.

"Don't talk bleedin' daft mate", she said. "She's on the assistance".

Bell gave the window another bang, and Peterson rattled the door handle. It was unlocked and the door swung inwards.

"I suppose you wouldn't care to accompany us whilst we go in and have a look around would you?", Peterson called to the woman above. "You know, just to be on the safe side, in case something is wrong".

"Not me mate", the fat woman said. "I minds me own business. Don't want nuffink to do wiv anyfink like that". She remained leaning over her window ledge; large, cow-like udders drooping over the edge, embraced by a dirty, well stretched greying blouse.

Bell turned to his companion. "Come on Bill", he said. "let's go in and see what gives, never mind that old cow".

"What's that?", crowed the fat woman overhearing the remark.

"Balls", muttered Bell, and they walked in and closed the door behind them.

Inside the basement, the air was stale and there was a familiar and acrid smell in the room. The fireplace was filled with ashes, and used cigarette butts littered the floor and fire hearth. The stench was unmistakeably that of cannabis. It was not surprising that the place was used for pot smoking. The main room was littered with old newspapers and empty baked bean cans. A plate on the table held a piece of meat at least a week old, covered in flies. Used coffee stained cups were left on tables and chairs, and on the mantle over the fireplace, together with empty wine bottles.

The room was dominated by a single divan bed, still unmade and with greying sheets covered by an old army blanket. Women's underwear littered the floor and corners of the room. A galvanised bucket on the floor in a corner, slowly filled as water dripped constantly from a wet patch in the ceiling where a toilet leaked on the floor above.

"My Christ!", breathed Bell. "Some bloody people...."

"Animals", corrected Peterson.

Bell moved towards a door at the back of the room, and opened it. A small kitchenette, equally as squalid and dirty as the main room. Nothing of interest there. He saw another door leading off the kitchen, towards the back of the premises. He opened the door and found himself in the toilet. The pedestal was cracked and unflushed. He opened the door a little wider and felt it come up against something which prevented him from opening it fully. He poked his head around the edge of the door and momentarily jumped with the sudden shock of seeing a girl lying in a crumpled heap against the wall behind the door. Both knees were drawn tightly up into her chest. Thin arms wrapped around her legs as if in pain. She was very pale and her face was twisted in agony. Her eyes were wide open, fear showing as she trembled and shook uncontrollably. She was oblivious of her visitors.

"Bill, quick", called Bell, moving deftly into the room and squeezing behind the door. Peterson joined him.

"What's up?", he said, rushing in from the main room where he had been sorting out cupboards and looking under the mattress.

"She's here", snapped Bell. "Looks bloody rough too".

Together they lifted the girl out and carried her into the main room where they dropped her onto the bed. The girl rolled and twisted her agonised body, and groaned frighteningly.

"What the hell's the matter with her?", said Peterson, unable to fully appreciate the situation.

"Poor bitch", muttered Bell. "Haven't you ever seen anyone suffering from withdrawal symptoms before. This kid's a junkie, and it looks very much to me like she needs a fix, and sharpish".

"Hell", breathed Peterson.

Bell took the girl's arm and pushed her sleeve right up. There were tiny pin pricks covering the crease at the elbow, and a line of similar red marks all down the forearm, tracing the course of the various veins. Some of the spots were vicious and turning septic through unhygienic needles and equipment. Her face was drawn and haggard, and she was dirty and unkempt. She wore just a long sleeved jumper over a pair of blue nylon panties. Nothing more.

Bell looked around. "Syringe", he said. "Have you seen a syringe about the place?"

"No", replied Peterson. "Haven't seen one".

"What's behind that toilet door. She may have been trying to give herself a fix in there".

Peterson hurried into the toilet and looked around.

"Nothing", he called.

"Right, get up to the car and radio for an ambulance right away. This kid needs help and fast".

Peterson dashed out and sprinted up the dirty steps to the street. He slid behind the wheel of the estate car and grabbed the handset of the radio. Quickly and efficiently he put out the call for an ambulance, then dashed back to assist his colleague.

"Ambulance is on its way", he said, puffing slightly. "Shouldn't be too long".

"Fine", said Bell, holding the girl's wrist, trying to keep account of her pulse. He slapped her face gently and tried to make contact with her. She just stared and trembled but said nothing.

"What the hell makes them do it?", Peterson said, looking at the girl. "I just can't understand it".

"I don't suppose we ever will know just what makes them do it", said Bell, sadly. "They have everything going for them these days, yet they want to just go and kill themselves, slowly and painfully, without any kind of dignity - for what? I wish I knew".

They stood staring at the unfortunate girl as she writhed on the bed. She couldn't have been more than nineteen at the most; although she looked older, that was the drugs. Her hair, once a golden mass of curls, was now lank and unwashed, lifeless and straight. Her eyes, once a shiny blue, were now dull, sunken and ringed with dark shadows, staring out of a gaunt, drawn face of grey taut skin. She was thin and under nourished. It had been a long time since she had bathed. A silver coloured chain and disc on her left wrist identified her simply as 'Penny'.

"So this is Penny Whiteman", sighed Bill Peterson.

"Do you know where she comes from?", asked Bell. "Has she any folks living around here?"

"I don't know", replied Peterson. "I'll see what the Collator has on her in the files. There must be something".

"What about that boyfriend of hers? Does he take junk too?", asked Bell.

"Don't think so", replied Peterson. "He runs with the yobbos, but I don't think he's on this kind of caper".

"Well, we'll have to find him and have a chat with him, won't we".

The siren was wailing and getting louder and Bell sent Peterson up to the street to show the ambulance attendants the way. He stayed with the poor girl, his heart filled with pity and compassion for the misguided creature on the bed.

"How long?", he wondered, "has she got before she just curls up and dies. How long, before her mind ceases to function at all, and her frail body just gives up the fight - for what? How the hell can we ever get the message over to them?; but they always think they know best. You can tell them and prove your theories to them, but still they think they know all the answers; and although you're absolutely right, you lose in the end because you didn't make them believe you - and you see them die". Bell pondered the misfortunes of life and sighed.

"In there", Peterson said, pushing the door open wide for the ambulance men. A stretcher wasn't going to be much use with the steps.

"We'll have to carry her up then", said the first attendant.

He stooped over the girl and looked at her eyes and then felt her feeble pulse.

"We'll have to hurry with this one", he said. "Any idea what she's on?"

"Heroin, I should think", drawled Bell. "Pretty advanced too, I'd say".

The ambulance men carried the girl up the steps and lifted her into the waiting ambulance, now surrounded by a couple of dozen women and kids. Women with cigarettes dangling from their loose, ugly mouths, arms folded across bra-less busts with skirts bursting at the zips, exposing dirty underwear. Old and young floozies, babbling to each other and exchanging the latest gossip. This at least, would keep them going for a while. What exaggeration would develop from this story - it would be something, quite something.

The doors closed and the ambulance men climbed aboard. The vehicle raced off with its siren blaring, towards the hospital. Bell and Peterson stood watching it disappear.

"What 'appened to 'er then mate?", came the inevitable question.

The crowd surged around the two Detectives, hoping to hear the full, sordid story. Bell looked around at the faces in the crowd.

"She got sick", he said, noncommittally, "that's all".

Chapter 9

Jimmy Bunce winced as he saw the two Detectives coming towards him in the White Cow cafe. He didn't like coppers and he was frightened of them when they wore plain clothes. He hadn't any good memories of his contact with the law in the past.

"James Bunce?", said Bell, sitting down at the table. Peterson stood behind Bunce, causing him to keep looking round nervously.

"Yeah, that's me", said Bunce with a sneer. "What you want?"

"When did you last see Penny?", said Bell.

"What's it to you?", replied Bunce.

"I'm asking", snapped Bell. "Now when did you last see her?"

"Yesterday morning", the youngster said. "Why?"

"You normally sleep with her don't you?", asked Peterson.

"Well, yes sometimes, but we 'ad a row yesterday morning and I walked out".

"What did you fight over?"

"Nuffink much, you know - money and fings".

"What things?"

"Well - she wanted me to get her some money for - well for spending like, you know".

"You mean money for junk?", said Bell.

"What do you mean, junk?", said Bunce innocently.

"Drugs, Bunce - drugs. You knew she was main-lining, didn't you?", Bell hissed. "Were you getting the stuff for her?"

"No guv'nor. I didn't have anything to do with her drugs".

"You knew she was on it though?"

"Well yes. 'course I knew, but I don't push junk myself and I had nuffink to do wiv 'er taking it".

"Why did you fight yesterday?"

"We didn't fight yesterday - well, not exactly fight. Just rowed 'cos I told her I wasn't going to keep givin' her money to chuck away on muck".

"Did she tell you she needed a fix?"

"She always needs a fix. That was the trouble. Every time I went there, she was ranting on about another fix and where was she going to get the money for more stuff. I didn't see the sense in chucking me money about like that. So, when she asked me for more money yesterday, I told her I wasn't goin' to give 'er no more money, and I said I was finishing wiv 'er".

"And what then?"

"Well, she kind of begged me to get her some money and go and find a pusher. Well, I might be a bit of a villain, but I ain't no drug-pusher. I don't want nuffink to do with that kind of fing. So I walked out and said I was finished wiv 'er. That was just before the pubs opened yesterday morning".

"Have you not seen her since?"

"No".

Bell sat quietly looking at Bunce, his face a dead pan. Peterson pulled a chair out and sat also. Their conversation was drowned by the noisy juke box anyway.

"Anyway", Bunce went on, "what's all this about then. What's wrong?"

"Who was she getting her stuff from, Jimmy?", Bell said at last. "You must know that much".

"I dunno, I swear. I never 'ad nuffink to do wiv that kind of fing. Sure, I gave 'her money, and I knew she was getting drugs wiv it, but that wasn't my business was it?"

"Who was her supplier?". Peterson leaned forward and grabbed Bunce by the lapel. "You're going to tell us - now talk".

"Look mate - I told you, I don't bloody know".

"Then you will try to find out, won't you old son?", said Bell, eyes narrowing menacingly.

"Well, what's happened then?", the lad said.

"Oh", replied Bell casually. "She's in hospital. She may even be dead by now".

Bunce went a ghastly white. He stood up and sat down again, his weakened legs unable to support his shocked body.

"Christ!", he whispered. "How?"

"Your money has bought her a one-way ticket", Peterson said with a sneer. "She's had too much heroin, I guess".

The two Detectives stood up and walked out of the cafe, leaving Bunce to think about his girl. He was shocked, that was clear, and frightened too, that the Police might blame him for whatever fate had done to Penny.

It was eight o'clock when Bell walked into the hospital ward. He had left Peterson to chase up a burglary in a solicitor's office. The Ward Sister showed him into the side ward where Bell saw Penny, now sitting up in bed with the aid of a back rest. She appeared tired and weak. She looked up as he came in.

"Hello, Penny", said Bell, cheerfully. "How do you feel now?"

"Who are you?", said the girl distrustfully.

"I'm Harry Bell. I found you this afternoon and got you into hospital. I'm a Policeman".

"Oh", the girl said, lowering her eyes. "I suppose I'm going to get another lecture now then, and then I suppose you want to charge me?"

"No", said Bell. "No lectures and no charges. I just want to talk to you and help you".

"Sure, they all say that. They all pretend to be so nice, and so...... so friendly, and say they want to help you, but all the time, what they really want is your confessions".

"I'm different", said Bell, softly and seriously. "I just want to talk. If you want me to help you, then I will. If you don't - well, okay, I won't. But you can help me if you won't help yourself; and you can help hundreds of other kids in your position. That's why I'm different Penny. I'm not going to force myself upon you. You know your position quite well and there's no point in arguing about it with you any more than the other people have already done. You can help yourself if you want to - and I'll help you to do it - if you want me to. The choice is entirely yours. In the meantime, I'd just like to talk about it".

Penny looked at him. She had never met a copper like this one before. She had been used to being pushed around a bit, from shop doorways late at night or moved on from the parks. She had been used to strict 'we know better than you' types at the probation office and social welfare. But this man really was different. He looked kind but at the same time, a hard man. He had seen a bit of life, that was obvious by his tone and his approach. He was no conman.

"How did you come to find me when you did?", she asked.

"I went with a colleague to interview you about another matter, but never mind that now".

"And you broke in?"

"The door was unlocked".

"Why did you go in?"

"Just had a feeling. You know, something tells you something is wrong".

"Are your instincts always right?", the girl asked.

"No. Wish they were. But sometimes, you get this feeling, you know - you can't explain it really. But when you get that feeling, you've got to follow it up. Well, I didn't like the feeling I had when we went to your place. So, we went right in".

"Well, I'm glad you did", Penny said softly. "Thank you mister. I guess you saved my life".

"Do you want to live then?"

"I don't want to die".

"Where are your parents Penny?"

"I have none. Car crash three years ago. I was left all alone at sixteen".

"Sorry".

"Don't be. It's not your fault. Daddy was drunk and drove straight into a lorry, head on. All the family was in the car, except me - I was at home".

"What happened to you after that?"

"I got turned out of the house and found digs in town. I got a job in the supermarket, but after a while, I got the sack for being absent too often. I just couldn't face the world some days, and stayed home in bed".

"No friends?", said Bell.

"I met a few, you know - down at the milk bar, and at the disco; but they weren't really interested in me as a person. I don't suppose many of the kids are really interested in each other. Anyway, I met a girl who introduced me to some friends one night, and we all went back to her place for a party. It lasted all night and someone persuaded me to smoke pot. I was sick at first, but after a few times, I got used to it. Gave me a kind of easy feeling, you know, made me lose my inhibitions and things. I woke up next morning in bed with a big West Indian fellow. He must have been fifty. After that, I just kind of mooched around with the crowd. We smoked pot quite regularly and had lots of parties and I began to enjoy myself. I thought I could handle things okay".

Bell took the girl's hand and looked at it, so small and thin - her bones showed through and the veins protruded like on an old lady. He looked at her sad face and choked back the lump in his throat.

"How did you get on to main-lining, Penny?"

"Yeah. Main-lining. God, I wish I had never started. We were having this party one night in a guy's house in London. We'd all gone down there for a big celebration party. Someone knew someone who had a cousin who was getting married, or something like that. Anyway we all went off in a half a dozen cars - I think they were all pinched from the car parks. We were having a great time until this geezer starts chatting me up about drugs. He asked me if I had ever tried anything other than pot. I told him no, and he said I should try this white stuff. Just pop it, he said; just prick the surface of your skin and skim a drop under the surface. Skin-popping he called it. He kept on and on, and in the end, I said okay. He filled a syringe and just pricked the surface of my arm and then squirted some into me. I felt funny after a while, and then passed out. I don't really know what happened then, but the next morning, I felt pretty miserable and this fellow was still around. He said what I needed was another pop. So he injected some more, just under the skin, like before. I didn't really feel any better. I was felling ill in fact, all day. He gave me some tablets and said they would make me feel much better. I found I had lots of energy and didn't give a hang about anything. From then on, I just drifted in and out of parties, and whenever someone offered to pop my arm, I agreed; but soon, I found that it wasn't so easy. I found that I was longing for another pop, and then one night, when a chap was popping me, he said, 'why don't you main-line?". I knew that that meant putting it directly into the blood stream. I had seen other kids do it. He said it would work faster. So I agreed. I've been properly hooked ever since, and each fix becomes more and more important. I became completely dependent on it, and my life became completely governed by the next fix. I went without food so I would have enough money to buy more stuff. People told me that I was a fool, but like all the others, I wouldn't listen. I thought I knew all the answers, until it was too late, then I only felt bitterness".

Penny dabbed at her dark eyes and sniffed. She stared at the clean white sheets, and her fingers twisted and worked rapidly. Bell remained silent. He just looked at this poor girl who's misguided life had almost ended that afternoon, because no one had really cared enough. She looked suddenly up at him.

"Well", she said. "I've told you the story now. I don't know why I should tell you. But now you know".

"Thanks", replied Bell, softly. "I'm flattered that you should confide in me this much." He smiled, and Penny grabbed his hand where it rested on the bed.

"I'm not going to die am I, Mister Bell?", she said desperately. There was fear in her voice.

"I hope not Penny", said Bell. He didn't know what else to say.

They both sat in silence for a while, not quite knowing what to say to each other. Bell finally took the initiative.

"Do you want to help me, Penny?", he said, optimistically.

"How?", said the girl, turning to look at him.

"You could start by telling me where the stuff comes from", he said.

"I don't know if I can", Penny replied, cautiously.

"Why not?"

"It might be bad for me".

"You mean they might come after you?"

"Yes".

"I'll make sure they won't", Bell said.

"How can you be sure?"

"Because, if you finger the pushers, I'll put them away for a long time", he promised.

"I don't know", Penny said, uncertainly. "I want to help, Mister Bell, but you know how it is".

"Look", said Bell. "We can get you officially registered as an addict, and get you into a nursing home for a cure - it'll be up to you to cooperate and it won't be at all easy, but you can be cured with patience and determination. You'll be out of the way and no pusher is going to get within a mile of you".

"I don't know.... I don't like hospitals".

"Do you prefer the mortuary?", Bell said, cruelly.

Penny wept bitterly. She cried and the tears ran down her thin face and onto the clean white, hospital sheets. She shook with fear and sobbed like a baby as she openly called upon God to save her from death.

Bell felt sick. Sick because here was a young thing in the prime of youth, yet as near to death as an old woman who had seen through four score years. He felt extreme pity which turned into hatred for the bastards who preyed upon these innocent kids in order to line their own pockets. He boiled up inside in the knowledge that a generation of fools were slowly killing each other off, for the sake of money and self satisfaction. It was worse than the war. At least in a war, there was some reason; some logic cause; some degree of patriotism and honour. But in this foul and degrading racket, there was nothing but shame and ghoulish greed and sorrow.

"Let me find the people responsible, Penny", Bell said. "Please - let me help to save somebody else."

"And what about me?", Penny sobbed.

"You'll be alright - I'll see to that", Bell promised.

The girl fell silent for a while. She blew her nose and settled down. Finally, she made up her mind. Whatever happened to her wasn't so important to her any more. She thought about the other kids at the disco, or at the schools and in the milk bars. All of them, trying to keep up with the others, doing what they stupidly thought was expected of them in order that they should not be branded as 'squares'; what fools.

"What do you want to know, Mr. Bell?", she said at last; quietly and resignedly.

"Good girl", breathed Bell, smiling at her kindly. "Just tell me who sells you the stuff and where I can find him. Where he gets his supplies from, if you know. You know, things like that".

"Alright then", she took a deep breath. "I buy heroin from Roger Bender. He's a guy about twenty-five. Hangs about at the Black Cat disco in town. You know the place?"

"I know it", said Bell, nodding.

"Well, he's about five feet eleven, big build and has long black hair. Always wears a smart suit. Got a way with the girls he has. He's there most nights from about nine o'clock onwards".

"Do you always get your supplies from him?

"Yes. I did get some a couple of times from another guy down there when Roger was away, but I don't know who he is. I think he works with Roger in the same line".

"Don't you know his name?"

"No".

"Alright. What else can you tell me?"

"Nothing really".

"What about these parties you always get in on? Where is the next one?"

"Well, you know, we just used to have a party when we felt like it. No one seemed to arrange them, they just seemed to happen".

"So there isn't one arranged then?"

"Well, as a matter of fact there is. Real swinger, coming off on Friday night at Benny Marshall's place".

"Where does he live?"

"He's got a cottage just outside the town, near the airport. You know that big old white Tudor place just before you reach the airport gates?"

"Yes, I know the place", said Bell.

"Well, he lives up there. I went there to a party once; fabulous".

"Who goes?"

"Everyone - just everyone".

"How do I get an invitation?"

"You just arrive".

"Fine". Bell paused. "Will Roger Bender be there?"

"He might be".

The Ward Sister came in with a syringe and medicine. She busied herself about the table on the other side of the bed.

"I think you had better make that all for now, Officer", she said. "This young lady has to rest".

"Alright", said Bell, standing. "Good luck, Penny. I'll see you again tomorrow, perhaps".

Penny just smiled and closed her eyes. She half lifted a hand as if to wave, and dropped it heavily on the bed again. Bell retreated silently.

Chapter 10

Bell found himself hooked on this case. It wasn't really his case at all, but he decided that he was going to make it his responsibility. He could, he knew, hand it over to the drugs squad. After all, they were the experts and knew what they were doing. But he wanted to play a major part in tracking down, and putting these evil men away. He wanted to avenge poor Penny's desperate predicament, so he spent the next couple of days scouting around the bars and discotheques, hoping to pick up some information which might prove useful in his task.

On the Friday night, he climbed into his old Austin and headed away from home. He was officially off duty and wore a casual shirt and slacks. He didn't know what to expect or whom he might see at the Marshall place. However, he listened to his old car radio as he drove up the long hill towards the airport. He turned onto the main road and switched his headlights on full. It was dark, about nine thirty, and he tried to get into the party mood so as to fit in. He stopped at the Devonshire Tavern and went inside. He drank two double scotches with soda, and then got back into the car.

"That should give it a bit of a start", he thought, as he started up and drove out onto the road again.

The large white, Tudor place was really three old terraced cottages built into one. The house had been renovated a few years previous. It looked impressive enough and a wide drive led around the house in an arc to a large yard at the rear. Two double gates afforded access.

As Bell pulled in, he saw that there was already a number of large cars parked both in the drive and around the back. Lights shone from just about every window in the house, and already, music drifted from within.

A noisy crowd of young men and girls jumped from a mini-bus and virtually danced their way across the drive and in through the large open front door above which hung an expensive coach lamp.

Bell locked his car and took a deep breath.

"Here we go then", he said to himself, making towards the door. He stepped gingerly through the door and was immediately greeted by a rather beautiful brunette with a very low-cut gown exposing most of her ample bosom. The gown, floor length, fitted tightly to her slender body and her eyes shone brightly in the half light of the hall. She had a champagne glass in one hand and a hand rolled cigarette in the other. The unmistakeable smell of cannabis filled the hallway and irritated Bell's nostrils.

"Hello good looking", the girl cooed. "What's your name then?" Her voice was silky, smooth and cultured. She had class and looks. She took Bell by the arm and led him towards a large room at the end of the hall.

"I'm Harry", Bell said, smiling. "What's yours?"

"Call me Janie", she said, flashing her eyes at him.

"Fine", said Bell.

They entered a very large room in which dozens of people stood around with drinks in their hands. Music played loudly from a stereo at the far end. The room was luxuriously furnished, and Bell wondered just what Benny Marshall's line was.

"I'll have to look him up in records", he thought.

They went over to a bar and Bell approved of the selection of drinks available.

"Whoever is paying for this lot has plenty of cash to chuck away", he thought. He helped himself to a glass of Chivas Regal. He could never afford to buy such quality whisky himself. He had been told by connoisseurs that there was none finer. So he took this wonderful opportunity to sample it free of charge.

"Cheers", he said, lifting his glass and chinking it against that in Janie's hand.

"Cheers", she echoed, and they drank.

Hey handsome, you want to dance?". A hand touched Bell on the shoulder and he looked around into the beautiful black face of a

West Indian girl. Her smile was full of whiteness and the plunging dress revealed full heaving breasts. The ankle-length dress was open to the hip exposing a long, beautifully shaped leg and the scarcest glimpse of pink panties. She wore no bra.

"Come on man", she coaxed, smiling all the time. "I might take a bite out of you from time to time, but I ain't no cannibal - come on, dance eh?"

He put his glass down on the mantlepiece and faced the girl, swaying already to the beat of a Caribbean rhythm. Bongo drums and the sounds of a steel band, throbbed and filled the room with excitement. Bell followed her out towards the middle of the floor, trying to match her movements in an awkward self conscious way. The girl smiled all the time and her looks excited him.

"What's yo name man?", asked the black girl, rocking and weaving.

"Harry", he replied. "What's yours?"

"Me?. I'm Ruby Masterson".

"Nice to meet you, Ruby?", said Bell.

The crowd in the room had opened up and were forming a large circle as the two danced to the ever increasing rhythm of the bongo drums. Bell swayed and copied Ruby's movements, and they gyrated and twisted, swayed and rocked. Bell couldn't take his eyes off his partner. Her long, black, shining legs flashed as she arched over backwards, and her well formed bosoms bobbed within the thin garment until her left breast actually popped right out for all to admire. Ruby allowed it to stay that way for several seconds before casually tucking it back inside her dress. She smiled at Bell as she did so, and winked.

"Hey man", she said, "you dig this music fine. I guess you make a good partner in bed too, uh?" and she laughed. Bell smiled a little shyly and chuckled.

"I wouldn't mind that so much", he said to himself, and Ruby seemed to read his thoughts.

"Mebbe later", she said, laughing still.

The music ended abruptly and Bell stopped dancing and took a deep breath. The rhythm had made him breathless. He noticed that there were quite a few black faces in the crowd and already some of the people were looking a little glassy-eyed. He walked to the mantlepiece and retrieved his glass of Chivas Regal. Ruby stood with him and sipped from his glass. She screwed up her face.

"Man, you go for whisky? Me, I like West Indian rum. Hey George, fetch me a Caribbean Special would you?"

A tall, dark skinned man nodded from the bar, and a few seconds later, made his way through the crowd towards them.

"Here Ruby", he offered, "as you like it".

"Cheers George", she said, "meet Harry".

"Hi man", said George.

"Hi George", replied Bell offering his cigarettes around. Ruby looked at him.

"They the best you have?", she asked.

"What's wrong with them?", said Bell, a little indignantly. He had bought a packet of the most expensive brand before coming that night.

"Well", said Ruby. "They ain't got no kick, like - you know, they can't turn a gal on".

"No", said Bell. "Well, they're all I've got".

"Well, mebbe later you'll burn a joint man", said Ruby winking.

"Yeah", said Bell.

Someone called to Ruby from across the room, and she excused herself and walked away. Bell watched her go and his eyes fixed on her swaying bottom as she walked.

"You fancy her, don't you?", said the silky voiced Janie, joining him.

"She's got something", said Bell, smiling at her.

"That depends on what you mean", said Janie, "But then, perhaps I'm a bit prejudiced".

"Well, she is different, you must agree", said Bell, lifting his drink to his lips.

"You married, Harry?", Janie asked.

"Yes", he said.

"Sure, I can normally tell the married ones".

"How's that then?"

"Oh, I don't know. They seem just a little bit on guard somehow. Can't put a finger on it exactly, but somehow, they seem to be looking out for a trap".

"You could be right", Bell replied, smiling. There was a pause in their conversation, then.

"You still smoking joints, Janie?", Bell asked.

She showed a little surprise. "What makes you think I smoke them at all?"

"You had one on when you met me at the door".

"Clever man", she said. "Don't you use them?"

"Nope. Where do you get them. Do they dish them out here then?"

"Some bring their own and push them around at a few bob a joint. Then we might get lucky and have a visit from a trader later on, we usually do".

"Who's that then?"

"No names, no comebacks", she said. "Why the interest. No one usually bothers who brings the stuff, just so long as it is available".

"Just curiosity", Bell said, and he decided to shut up.

The party raved on and became more and more relaxed. People danced, and by midnight, several of the women were stripped down to their panties as they danced. Black and white paired off together, and some disappeared up the stairs. Bell tried to keep his drinking to a minimum, but found it almost impossible since girls kept plying him with drinks and offering to recharge his glass.

"You're not one of the usual crowd, are you?", a good looking woman of around thirty joined him. "I mean, you don't usually come to the parties".

Bell looked at the woman and immediately recognised her as Gloria Vance, a pretty high class prostitute from the other side of town. He had seen her a couple of times in Court, once when she appeared on a charge of keeping a brothel, and another time when she was a witness for the defence in a case of an illegal abortion.

"Hello Gloria", he said. "Nice to see you".

Gloria was taken aback. She had thought that she had smelt out an intruder, but was surprised to find that he knew her and wondered from where.

"We've obviously met before", she said, "you must be..."

"Harry", replied Bell. "Sure, we've met before, probably at one of the parties".

Gloria was surprised. She didn't usually forget a face and she was pretty sure that she had not met this man socially before. It bothered her a little.

"Well", she said "Enjoy yourself. See you around."

"Yeah", replied Bell, grinning. "See you".

It was getting hot and the atmosphere was thick and humid. Smoke filled the room and the acrid smell of cannabis was prominent. Bell realised that the stuff was being used quite openly and he hoped that the drugs squad wouldn't turn up suddenly and find him there. He would never be able to explain away his presence. He thought about Sue, down on the coast with her mother. What would she have said if she had known he was a guest at a drug orgy? He shrugged. He hoped things would turn out alright and that he could have her home soon.

Chapter 11

About twelve-thirty there was a bit of a commotion in the hall, and Bell realised that a new arrival had appeared. There was general discussion between the new arrival and Benny Marshall. Then the new man went out to the drive and took a small case from the boot of a car. He came back into the house and went up the stairs. Marshall moved amongst the guests muttering quietly to each in turn. Some disappeared up the stairs, extracting wallets as they went. Marshall avoided Bell. He took no chances with people he didn't recognise. Bell decided to make a few casual enquiries himself about the new arrival. He collared Ruby as she flitted across the room towards the bar.

"Hey Ruby", he said. "What gives with the guy upstairs? Everyone seems to be clearing off up there after him".

"Man, you mean you don't know our Roger? Why, he sells the inner soul man, life for them who don't have the real life for free. Me, I don't need it, but you know man, there's a lot of people who like to buy a few grains of oblivion occasionally. Roger merely comes and fulfils their needs".

"Oh, yes sure", said Bell, trying to hide his obvious interest.

"Me", continued Ruby, "I get my kicks out of people, you know - men, all kinds of men, but mostly I like big, strong men, and I like 'em best in bed, you know. Are you like that, Harry?"

Bell grinned and winked, put his glass to his lips and evaded the question.

He decided to go straight to Roger Bender in the bedroom. He wanted to catch the man with some of the stuff on him. He also wanted to find out more about his supplier. He chose a suitable moment to disappear, and then sprinted up the stairs towards the door where a light shone beneath the bottom end. He opened the door and walked in.

Bender was just injecting a young girl with heroin. He was main-lining her and she was far away and dreamy. A heap of notes lay on the bed beside the case which contained several more packets of heroin, several bottles of pills and one or two chunks of cannabis. He looked up as Bell entered the room and his mouth dropped. He whipped the syringe out of the girl's arm and patted her. She got up and left. Bell walked over to him.

"Alright Bender", he said. "This is the end of the line for you old son". He flashed his Police Warrant card and made a grab for the suitcase. He snapped the lid closed and grabbed the bundle of notes and stuffed them in his pocket.

"You're under arrest for illegal possession of this stuff, he said. He made a grab at Bender who shouted for Marshall.

The door flew open and Marshall came in together with four other men. They were big men, two West Indians and two Englishmen.

"What's the trouble?", said Marshall, politely. "Is everything alright?" He was addressing Bell.

"He's the bleedin' law", started Bender, shaking in his shoes.

Marshall looked sharply at Bell. "Who are you Mister?" he said. Bell withdrew his warrant card again and showed Marshall.

"I'm a Detective Officer", he said, "and I am arresting this man for possessing illegal drugs. I am also placing you under arrest for allowing your house to be used for smoking cannabis and for aiding and abetting this man in the illegal distribution of drugs. I must caution you..."

"That will be enough, Mister", snapped Marshall. "I don't think you are going to arrest anyone, in fact you are drunk and don't know what you are saying".

Bell made a move towards Bender and the four men came at him and grabbed him. They carried him into another room where they dropped him onto a bed.

"Bring me a sleepy drink", ordered Marshall, "For our guest".

Bell knew that it would do no good to try to fight his way out of this one. He just had to play it their way for the time being. He lay back on the bed and the four men held him down. Minutes later,

Ruby came in, together with Janie and Gloria; Ruby carried a glass of what appeared to be whisky.

"Drink this", ordered Marshall, handing the glass to Bell.

"I'm not thirsty", said Bell.

"Drink it", said Marshall, grabbing Bell by the hair and yanking his head backwards. Ruby poured some of the liquid into Bell's open mouth and he swallowed automatically. She repeated the process twice more until the drink was all gone.

"Alright", she said. "You can all go now".

The men turned and left the room, and Bell realised that he could not move. The drink had been drugged and he was helpless.

"What was that bloody stuff?", he growled.

"It's quite harmless", replied Ruby. "It's only a knock-out powder. It won't hurt you".

"You're all in this together aren't you?", Bell said, shaking his head which had already become hazy.

"Quiet now", said Ruby. "We're going to give you a nice time, aren't we girls?"

Bell opened his eyes and saw that Ruby had slipped the dress of and was standing over him, wearing only the delicious pink panties. Gloria Vance was stepping out of her dress and the beautiful Janie was unzipping the back of her gown too.

"Christ!", thought Bell, "a bloody orgy and I can't bleedin' move".

Ruby was now kissing him all over and the other two women were doing things to him which completely overpowered his sexual control. He wished that he could move and at least enjoy the orgy properly, but he could not control his limbs. The three women performed on him in the most expert and erotic manner and Bell knew that this must be their own special way of deriving pleasure. Eventually, he passed out and knew no more.....

Chapter 12

Mavis Jones, brothel-keeper, sat at the table with her current man. Frank Weymes lived with her and kept her as his wife as long as it suited him. Together they studied the photographs depicting three gorgeous women performing on a helpless Harry Bell on a bed. The pictures were good, and to anyone looking at them, it was clear that Harry Bell was enjoying the sexual deviations being performed by the three beauties.

"Great!", said Weymes, "But who is the guy?"

"He's a copper", replied Mavis. "He gate-crashed Benny's party on Friday and tried to arrest Roger with his consignment. Fortunately, Benny stopped him and the girls I had sent to the party, obliged by performing whilst Benny got busy with the camera. If it hadn't been for that, you wouldn't have got your money for that lot of stuff Roger got rid of. He'll have to be careful in the future though, Frank".

Weymes looked pensively at the pictures. "He's a copper, is he?"

"That's right".

"Local?"

"Yes", said Mavis, "but not on the drugs squad".

"Well we can use these no doubt. I'll take them and show the boss. He'll pay me well for them. He's always on the lookout for a copper he can bribe or corrupt. I reckon he'll have no bother with this one, eh?"

"Sure Frank", said Mavis.

Weymes put the pictures in his pocket and tapped his jacket. "I don't know how the man could have been so bloody foolish", he said. "See you tonight, love". and he kissed Mavis on the cheek and left.

Frank Weymes was the pushers' main supplier in the town, and he pulled many strings. Roger Bender was one of his pushers and did a good job for him. Weymes found no difficulty in recruiting pushers from the disco's, and in his position, ran little risk of detection himself. He worked for a top man who obtained the supplies from an unknown source, and distributed them throughout a vast and intricate network of middle men. Weymes was the top man next to....the boss.

Marshall was nothing in the organisation. He was a big-time, local businessman with a few criminal interests. He had contacts in the underworld who would pull strings for him when he needed favours. He had seen the opportunity of making a few pounds out of Bell's predicament and at the same time, getting into the good books of the big time boss. He had organised the photographic session and then, whilst Bell was still under the influence, had driven him home and put him to bed. It hadn't been difficult to find his address. His wallet had shown all they needed to know, and the front door key was, of course, on Bell's key ring. They had simply taken him home, put him to bed and left. Bell had awakened in his own bed, and with a heavy hangover from which he was suffering, he really didn't know whether he had dreamed all the events of the previous night, or not. But the love-bites on his body, told him that his recollection of the event must be pretty accurate.

"Christ!", he thought, "what a fool I've been. I should have called in the drugs squad right from the start". He moaned quietly. "I ballsed up that job proper".

Chapter 13

Chief Inspector Frost called Bell into his office and told him to shut the door. Bell sat down and waited for his Chief to address him. He supposed this was going to be one of those secretive little chats the governor had from time to time with his men.

"How's the warehouse jobs coming along then, Bell?" Frost said bluntly.

"Not too good Sir", Bell replied.

"Why not?", said Frost.

"Just don't seem to be getting any leads Sir, and anyway there seems to have been a bit of a lull in warehouse breakings just lately".

"Don't let that fool you, Bell. Just because no new breaks have been done recently, doesn't mean you can forget those that have already occurred, does it?"

"We cleared up most of them Sir".

"But we haven't got the big man yet, have we, Bell?" Frost hissed. "That's the man I want - the man at the top".

"I fancy Chandler for the top man, Sir", Bell said. "In fact, I'm certain of it - but how does one prove his complicity. He's shrewd and leaves nothing to connect him with these activities. I think he has interests in many other fields too, but I don't know just what".

"Well work on it", Frost said, signing a batch of reports on the desk in front of him. It looked like he had no more to say on the subject for the moment.

"Yes Sir", said Bell rising to his feet. "I'll see what I can do".

Bell went out to the main office and sat at his desk. He sorted out some more of his outstanding paperwork and submitted one or two files in readiness for Court proceedings. He was annoyed and frustrated at not getting a good line on Chandler.

"I'll have to fix him somehow", he thought, "even if I have to plant some evidence myself".

He spent the rest of the day doing the rounds of his informants again, urging them to get their ears to the ground and come up with something, anything they could, on the warehouse breakings. He desperately wanted to be in on the next job. He wished he knew the identity of the man who had given him the tip about the Harvey and Browns job - perhaps he could help. But it was hopeless.

He walked into the Locomotive bar for a beer. It was almost lunch time and he was dry.

"Hello Harry", said the barmaid. "Usual?"

"Please", said Bell, digging his hand into his pocket and extracting a note. "Have one yourself too, love".

The barmaid smiled and put his pint on the counter, rung up the till and gave him his change. She looked around and nodded him to the other end of the long bar. "Remember those radios and tellies you were talking about, Harry?"

"Yes, what about it?"

"Well, I've been offered a colour television for twenty-five quid, brand new".

"Aw, come off it", said Bell. "Twenty-five quid for a colour T.V. just ain't on. Blimey, that's ridiculous".

"Maybe, but that was the price offered, oh and perhaps a favour or two at the weekend - you know, a girl has to be grateful somehow", she winked.

"Ah, yes", said Bell philosophically. "Who and when?"

"A fellow I know, comes in here from time to time. He works at a big warehouse somewhere out of town. Radios, televisions, tape recorders and all that stuff you know, everything in that line".

"What's this chaps name then?"

"Don. Don Broadman. He's got a brother, smooth character but a bit of a rough-neck with women. Anyway, this Don chap, comes in quite often and I got talking to him. We got onto the subject of tellies etc, and I happened to mention that I wouldn't mind a nice colour set. Straight away, he says he can fix me up with one - for a small consideration - you know like. Anyway, I says "How much?", and he says, "Well for you, twenty-five quid, providing I get some special consideration over the weekends". I told him I live in a flat on my own".

"Well, that's your business", said Bell, "but how is he going to get the stuff?"

"Well, I gathered from what he was saying, that he is going to have a load away soon. He knows a lot of villains in town and it wouldn't be hard to get a few together to do the place now would it?"

"Any idea when?", Bell said, hopefully.

"He said he'd give me a ring when he was ready to drop me a set, so I would be ready for him".

"Alright", said Bell. "Here's my telephone number - office and home. Ring me as soon as you know any more, I want Mr. Broadman and his mates with the gear - okay".

"Okay, Harry, but do I get a set or not?"

"I told you I'd fix it for you didn't I?", he replied. "Right, then I will".

"Sure Harry", she said. "Sure".

Bell left the Locomotive feeling very pleased with himself. He at least had a lead on a job yet to be pulled, and he was going to take advantage of that advanced knowledge. He hurried back to the Police Station and went to the Collator's office.

"Is he in?", he said to the little secretary typing in the corner.

"Who?", she said.

"Who do you think? - P.C. Smith. Is he about?"

"No, he's gone for lunch", the girl replied, "and I'm going too, right now".

"Can I help myself then?", Bell said, pulling open the filing cabinet drawer marked 'Nominal Index'.

"Be my guest", the girl said tartly, and she disappeared through the door, handbag in hand.

Bell thumbed through the cards until he came to the name 'Broadman'. The first was Colin. He stopped and read the file out of curiosity. This was the bastard who attacked Sue. He read on. 'Convictions for assault on Police, two previous for G.B.H. and one for indecent assault on a female'.

"Nice chap", said Bell aloud, replacing the card and extracting the next. 'Donald Broadman'. This one, it seemed, was previously known for theft and burglary. He had little form really, and the last conviction was some nine months previous for theft of a portable radio from a shop. He had been placed on probation for two years. Found to be living at a local doss house in Regent Street and working for 'Quality Sound Services', a wholesale distribution firm, specialising in televisions, radios, tape recorders and the like. Known associates - Ricky James, Bernard Smedley, Bimbo Parks and local layabouts in general.

"Well fancy that", murmured Bell, noting the relevant details. "What a select bunch".

He went out and hummed to himself as he ascended the canteen steps, two at a time. He ordered and ate a regular lunch and played a game of snooker with the lads in the games room. He felt pleased with himself and spent an hour or so taking things a bit easy.

That afternoon, Bell drove out to 'Quality Sound Services' and asked to see the Chief Security Officer, an ex-Detective Sergeant who once worked with Bell in the force.

Dan Dene was a big man with grey hair and warm blue eyes. He reached out his big hand to Bell and they shook warmly.

"What brings you out here then Harry?", the man said. "Anything we can do?"

"Yes", said Bell, "can we go to your office?"

They walked through the premises and into a large office on the gallery floor overlooking the entire storage area. Bell took a seat and accepted a glass of whisky from the filing cabinet.

"Cheers", toasted Dene, and they drank the whisky and recharged.

"What's your security like here, Dan?", asked Bell, seriously. "I mean alarms, locks and all that kind of thing". Dene looked at him, surprised.

"Fine", he said. "Our security is first class. All the doors and windows are adequately locked and alarmed. No one could get in here once the place is closed".

"What about someone getting out with a lorry load of gear - I mean, someone who shouldn't really be taking the stuff out at all?"

"We have checkers and tally men. Everything that moves is checked and tallied and the drivers get a clearance slip for each load. No one loads his own vehicle and no one knows what vehicle or load or destination he has until he actually received his tally slip. It's pretty tight, Harry".

"Sounds alright", said Bell.

"So what's your problem?", asked Dene.

"I think this place is going to get done, soon".

"How?"

"Don't know yet. But someone who works here is going to have some gear away".

"Who?"

"Sorry Dan, can't say - you know - it wouldn't do would it?"

"No, I suppose not", said Dene. "What can I do then?"

"I don't really know just yet", said Bell, scratching his head.

"What exactly are they going to steal then?", said Dene.

"I know they will have colour tellies at least".

"Ah!, well now, we don't carry any in stock at the moment. We're expecting a consignment from Japan soon, but we haven't got any right now. Are you sure that's what they're after?"

"Oh yes", said Bell "And a bloke who is after them actually works here".

"So he must know that we haven't got any in stock and that we're expecting them soon".

"Exactly".

"So?"

"So the chances are, he'll have them off before they actually come inside the premises".

"How?"

"Hijack the lorry, perhaps", said Bell.

"Christ! you could be right", retorted Dene.

"So who is your distributor?"

"I'll have to check up on that one", said Dene. "Give me a ring tomorrow morning. I'll find out who the importing agent is and who will be delivering".

"Fine", said Bell. "I think you and I will are going to have something to drink to again soon".

They refilled their glasses and drank each other's health once more.

"I'll ring you in the morning then", said Bell. "So long Dan".

"See you Harry", said Dene.

Chapter 14

It had been five days since Bell had found Penny Whiteman sick and almost dying in the house in Bourne Hill. He had meant to go back to visit her in hospital but just hadn't got around to it. He decided therefore, to pay her a visit after finishing duty that day, after seeing Dan Dene.

At seven o'clock that evening, having eaten at the little restaurant down the road, Bell started his old Austin and headed out towards the large hospital on the main road. He was feeling good. At last things seemed to be moving and he looked forward to getting on with the job. He stopped at a red traffic light and watched an old man hobble across the road. The man was a bit of a local character and Bell recognised him. The old man, hunched over onto his walking stick and dressed in a greasy old overcoat with an even longer old school scarf wrapped three times around his thin neck, looked up and saw Bell behind the wheel. Bell waved and called out a good evening.

"Evening Mr. Bell", replied the character, "nice to see you".

"Mind how you go Jim". Bell called back, and the old man succeeded in making the safety of the other side of the road before the lights changed to green again.

As he drove, Bell thought about Sue. "Really must write to her I suppose", he mused. "I should telephone her. I'll do that tonight, after I've been to the hospital". He thought on, "Funny though, I would have thought Sue could have phoned me by now. She's been gone long enough". He felt a pang of guilt for neglecting his wife, but then, resentment because she had not bothered to contact him, either.

He turned into the large hospital car park and looked for a suitable space. He locked up his old car, "Not that any fool would nick it", he chuckled. "I really must get myself a decent car one of these days".

Inside he spoke to a girl on the reception desk. She was pretty with dark hair and lovely eyes. Her mouth looked warm and inviting.

"Would I like to take her home?", he asked himself, leering inwardly.

"Can I help you?", the girl enquired.

"Yes please", replied Bell, absently. "Oh, er, yes, I'd like to visit Miss Penny Whiteman, Ward Twelve".

The girl looked in the register. "I'm sorry Sir", she said. "Miss Whiteman has been discharged".

"When?", asked Bell, surprised.

"Two days ago Sir", said the girl. Discharged herself against advice".

"Do you know why?", Bell queried.

"No Sir, but the Ward Sister might be able to help, you can go up if you wish".

"Thanks", said Bell. "I think I'd better".

He dashed up the stairs and arrived at Ward Twelve, out of breath.

"Good gracious", said the Sister. "You'll be having a heart attack young man if you dash around like that too much".

"Yes, I know", replied Bell. "What can you tell me about Penny Whiteman? I'm a Police Officer".

"Yes, I remember you", said the Ward Sister. "Penny decided to discharge herself. The doctor advised her to go into one of our clinics, but she said she could not face it. We tried everything but she wouldn't listen. I'm afraid we can't force people to have treatment if they don't want it".

"I can't understand it", Bell muttered, bewildered at the girl's change of attitude.

"It isn't unusual", said the Sister. "These people don't seem to be able to listen to reason. When they do and you think you're getting through to them, they suddenly let you down with a bang by changing their minds without any reason or logic. It's a terrible thing".

"Did anyone visit her?", asked Bell.

"No one at all".

"Where did she go?"

"I've no idea", said the Sister.

"I see. Thanks, sorry to bother you Sister, you must be busy".

"Not at all Officer", she said. "I wish I could help more".

Bell left the hospital feeling rather dejected and let down. He had felt sure that Penny would go into a drugs dependency clinic for a cure. He thought she had seen the light - how wrong he was. He climbed once more into the car and started the engine. He turned onto the main road again and headed for the G.P.O. A bank of telephones standing on the pavement were mostly full, but just one was vacant. Bell stepped inside and fumbled for his diary. He turned the pages and found the number, then dialled. He heard the number ring out and then a click. His mother-in-law spoke.

"Hello Ma", Bell said. "It's me, Harry - how are things down your end?"

"Oh, you haven't completely forgotten you've got a wife down here then", came the curt reply. "What kept you so long?"

Bell curled his lip and made a face at himself in the mirror, conveniently situated at nose level in the kiosk.

"Sorry about that", he said. "I've been terribly busy. How is Sue. Is she there?"

"Hang on", said his mother-in-law, "I'll call her".

Bell waited for a minute and then heard his wife's voice on the line.

"Hello Harry", she said, seriously.

"Hello sweetheart", he said. "How are you - I'm sorry I haven't phoned you before, but you just wouldn't believe how busy I've been".

"Oh, but I would Harry", she said sarcastically.

"Well, you could have phoned me Sue, couldn't you?"

"Oh, but I have Harry", she said. "Several times. I even phoned you last Friday night, six times in all, from eight o'clock until four in the morning, but you weren't at home Harry - where were you - in bed with someone else I suppose?"

"Oh Christ, not that again", he moaned.

"Well", she demanded, "where were you then?"

"I was working", Bell snapped.

"But I phoned your office at eleven o'clock that night, and they told me that you had booked off-duty at six.

"Well they were wrong", snapped Bell. He realised that he was, in fact, in bed with someone else, just like Sue said. But not just with one woman; it had been three at once. He felt guilty even though he had had no control over the situation. He hadn't gone to bed voluntarily with them, but then, would he have done so if things had been different? He guessed he would have done just that.

"Look Sue", he went on, "I'm working flat out on this bloody job to get you home with me again. Do you think I like having you away. I hate it. I'm trying my damnedest to get things to square up, and all you do is abuse me. I love you Sue, don't you know that?"

"I've heard that before", she replied. "Well go on - have a good time if that's what you want. You're more in love with your damned job than you are with me. Well just see if Mr. Bloody Frost is any comfort to you when you grow old and retire".

"Oh come on, Sue".

"No Harry, I've said enough and I'm tired. Goodnight".

The phone burred and Bell looked at it in disbelief. He replaced the receiver and stepped out into the night air.

"Damn women!", he cursed, and a middle-aged woman waiting at the bus stop looked at him with a frown on her face.

"I beg your pardon young man", she said, rather haughtily.

"Get stuffed", Bell snorted, and climbed back into the old banger. "So that's the way she wants it, is it?", he said to himself out loud. "What a bloody way to carry on. I don't know why I bother. How the hell do you get through to a woman. They're all the bloody same - pig-headed and stubborn - always know it all. Well, if that's how she wants it, she can have it that way". He drove with determination and pulled up outside the big, new 'Thistledown Hotel'. He parked the car, brushed his suit down with his hands and walked in.

The lounge bar was large and furnished with expensive fittings - a deep piled carpet silenced his footsteps as he made his way towards the bar. A double whisky soon disappeared and a second one replaced it on the bar. Leaning on the bar, he looked around at the faces of people drinking and talking. They were a mixed bunch, mostly couples and dinner parties awaiting tables in the restaurant.

Bell drank and reordered more whisky. He was already feeling the effects of the spirit. He felt warm and loosened his tie in spite of the odd look the barman gave him. He sat on the high stool and lit another cigarette.

"Hey man, put it there, nice to see you again", the voice behind him whispered. He turned and saw Ruby Masterson standing alone. She wore ordinary clothes and looked just as lovely as before. He grinned and offered to buy her a drink. She accepted and slid onto the stool beside him.

"Well Harry man, what makes you drown your sorrows here?"

"Women", Bell said. "Women".

"I thought you like women, Harry?"

"Well, wife trouble then".

"She gone away, Harry?"

"Yep".

"How long?"

"Long enough", said Bell.

"You want company Harry man - you need someone to talk to and bed with?"

"You kidding Ruby?"

"I thought last Friday, you enjoyed being with me?"

"I did, but you did me wrong, Ruby. You play a dangerous game".

"I liked it Harry".

"I might have liked it too, if you hadn't forced that sleeping powder on me. What was it all about anyway?"

"You just dreamin' Harry. You just fell asleep - drunk I guess".

"You know that's not true, Ruby"

"Can you prove different man?"

"I guess not - but I will one day".

"You want me tonight, Harry - just me - no one else. Huh?"

Harry Bell looked at the black Ruby. He fancied her, sure; but dare he accept such an invitation? "Why not?", he thought. "Who's to know?". But something inside told him not to give way to his desires too easily.... He wanted to find out what made such a girl tick. She sure knew how to make a man feel switched on, and she enjoyed life to its full, that was clear. She was alive and vital and beautiful, more beautiful than any other woman of her race he had ever seen.

"Come on Harry man", she said, coaxing him with her eyes and her lovely smile. "Come back with me and tell me your troubles man. I dig you plenty Harry, and I fancy tumbling you - in my bed".

"I'll say this for you Ruby. You say what you mean, don't you? You don't beat around the bush. I like you for that".

"Sure", she replied. "What's the point of beating the bushes when you can walk straight between them just as easy".

Bell looked on in silence, studying her eyes, the corners of her mouth, and the flash of white teeth as she smiled. "Where do you live Ruby?", he asked suddenly, tossing the last of his whisky down his throat.

"You got a car outside?"

"Sure - at least, an apology for a car".

"Okay, you drive - I'll show you where".

They left together and the patrons stared after them. Bell ignored them. They were, after all, only jealous. He opened the door for Ruby and she climbed in. She looked around.

"I thought they paid you guys more money than this", she said, nodding at the interior of the car.

"Yeah, well - one day I'll get around to changing it", Bell replied.

He drove on her instructions, until they came to a rather smart block of flats in what was once the slum district of town, but had been rebuilt and was now much improved. The well furnished flat was clean and neat. It was exciting just being there, alone with Ruby. He knew that he was being far from discreet, and could be asking for trouble, but somehow, he didn't care. He felt a compulsion to experience this woman. She was so warm, yet so carefree and beautiful. Such a body, he had not seen in many a long year; supple, yet firm and full.

"Come on in Harry", she said. "Help yourself to a drink over there".

Bell ambled across the large room to a cabinet and helped himself to a whisky.

"What about you?", he called, and she answered from the bedroom. "No thanks", she said.

"Well, good health", Bell said, and he tossed the drink down.

He walked to the bedroom door and leaned against the frame. Ruby was peeling off her dress and Bell felt the thrill of her exciting body across the room. She wore filmy white panties and a slim bra. Her legs were long and firm and shiny, and her waist, a tiny hourglass shape. A flat tummy with muscles rippling under the black shiny skin, fascinated him. He watched as she reached her hands behind her and unclipped the bra. The garment fell away and Bell felt an urge to rush over and cup her breasts in his hot hands.

Ruby looked up and saw his gaze. She smiled and winked devilishly, and Bell tried to control the heartbeats which had quickened.

"Well Harry", she began. "Here we are man. Are you going to spend the night propping up that wall, or are you going to come over here and do what you're thinking about right now?"

Bell straightened up. He reached into his pocket and withdrew a packet of cigarettes.

"Cigarette?", he offered.

"No thanks", Ruby said.

Bell lit the cigarette and drew in smoke. He looked at Ruby, now reclining on the bed, propped up on one elbow. She looked at him and tried to puzzle out just what it was that made this man so very different.

"What the hell am I doing here, Ruby?", Bell said at last. "Christ, I don't know what's happening to me. I seem to have got myself caught up in some high speed jet-set and I don't feel I belong here".

"You scared man?"

"What of?"

"Me perhaps. Because I'm black - is that it Harry? You're not too sure because I'm black woman - I'm different and you don't feel too sure. Yes, I guess that's it eh, man? Well let me tell you this. I'm no different from your wife or your other white women. Down under this skin, I'm just the same. Only perhaps I understand a little more about life and humility and people. Do you know why Harry? Do you know why I know more about life and people, than your white women do? Well I'll tell you. It's because I've had to learn to live with them in spite of myself. I'm black, but I'm not ashamed of it. I am black and I'm beautiful, and I'm cashing in. Being beautiful and black makes me kind of special. What is it you whites say? The blacks are either ugly or they're very beautiful. Well, I'm one of the beautiful ones Harry. But there are lots of people in this world who hate us because we're not the same as they are - white people Harry, people like you - do you hate me Harry?, do you hate us blacks, eh?"

Bell looked on admiring the girl. Her eyes wide and fiery, neck stretching forward as if to emphasise the sudden outburst. Her knuckles showed white through black skin as she clenched her fists tightly, a handful of bedclothes gripped in each.

"God she is certainly what she says", he thought.

"Ruby", he said at last. "I don't hate you or your people. I only hate those who exploit and degrade and ruin innocent youngsters. I don't care what colour they are. Some blacks are bastards, but no more than some whites are. Me? I don't bother about colour, just people. Sure Ruby - I'm uncertain about you, but not because you're black Ruby, oh no. I'm uncertain because I feel a desire for you and because I have a wife already. I'm no angel. I've kicked around a bit, but that was before I married. Okay, we're going through a bad patch and she's away right now. I want to make love to you like hell, Ruby, but I just feel bad about it. Yes, you're black and very beautiful and perhaps that makes my desire just that little bit more urgent and exciting - oh yes, exciting, Ruby. Just don't push me - okay?"

Ruby softened. Her grip on the sheets relaxed and the smile returned. She patted the bed and tossed her head, beckoning him to join her.

"Come here Harry", she whispered softly, her voice barely audible. Bell ambled across the carpeted floor and sat beside her on the bed. He looked down at her full figure as she reclined, still propped up on one elbow. Ruby took his hand and squeezed it.

"I'm sorry Harry", she said at last. "I guess you're a pretty nice guy after all. I always thought all coppers were natural bastards - inhuman and without souls. You, Harry - you're not like that at all. I guess you really do love that wife of yours, eh?"

"Ruby love, my wife is a long way off right now, and she doesn't feel too trustful of me. She seems to want to believe that I'm having it off with every woman I come into contact with. Well okay, let her believe it if she wants to. D'you fancy me Ruby? I mean, really fancy me; or do you just want to be able to say you slept with a white Detective - or maybe you want to compromise me and have someone burst in here in about two hours time and demand quiet money from me? What really is your angle Ruby?"

"You hurt me, Harry", she replied, pouting her lips. "That wasn't called for at all. I told you, I like you and I want to make love with you, just for you, not for any other reason. You turn me on Harry man. I dig you like crazy and I fancy you, okay?"

"Okay". Bell fell silent for a moment longer then he stood up and stubbed out his cigarette in the ash tray beside the bed. He looked once more at Ruby and pulled off his tie. She watched him, a tender look on her face. He threw his jacket on a chair and unbuttoned his white shirt, slowly and with deliberation. As he stripped off the shirt, Ruby realised that he was well tanned and his physique was good and well proportioned. He had looked after himself even though some of the muscle was a little soft here and there. She moved into the bed and pulled the sheets up around her shoulders, watching him all the time.

Bell walked to the bed, his only covering was the darkness of the room now that he had switched off the light. He pulled back the covers and fully exposed Ruby, lying there, silhouetted against the white sheets, black against white. Bell slid on to the bed beside her and bent over her. His left hand cupped one firm, full breast and he kissed the nipple lightly. His face moved towards her and her lips parted slightly as they met his. She put a slender arm around his neck and pulled herself against him as she responded to his kiss. Her body squirmed against his and he felt himself giving in completely to her exquisite passion and warmth.

Chapter 15

Dan Dene had been true to his word and had made the appropriate enquiries. When Bell telephoned him at ten o'clock the following morning, he had the answers ready.

"Our consignment of colour television sets are coming in via the 'Shipway Import and Export Company', Harry. The owner of the firm is a Johnathan Michaelson. They use their own transport under the name of 'Ocean Import Services Limited'. As far as I can ascertain, they're a straight firm".

"Okay Dan", said Bell. "When is the consignment due?"

"Don't know yet Harry. I'll give you the tip as soon as I know".

"Thanks Dan".

Bell returned to his morning paperwork. His desk just didn't seem to ever get clear.

"Bloody paper Empires, that's what it's all for", sighed Bell, rummaging through and checking.

That morning, he gave evidence in Court at the Committal hearing against Bimbo Parks for robbing the old tramp. The solicitor defending, accused Bell of planting the watch on his client and of mistaken identity. He tried all the tricks in the book to throw doubt into the minds of the Magistrates, but Bell was not deterred. He had experience all the dodges that solicitors sometimes used when there was no clear line of defence, before. Now, he stood in the witness box.

"I put it to you Officer", said the solicitor, "that what you saw in that alleyway on that dark night, was someone jumping over a wall. You did not see who that person was. You found the old man on the ground and picked up his watch which he had dropped in the struggle. You decided that the person you had seen going over the wall was a youth whom you thought you recognised, although you didn't see his face; and you went to the White Cow cafe and picked my client as your suspect. You went up to him and made a pretence of searching him and came up with the watch which you had taken in with you. Is that not right, Officer?"

"No Sir, that's a lot of nonsense", replied Bell, flatly.

"I submit that my client was not in fact in possession of that watch at all".

"He was swinging the chain blatantly when I walked in the place. I pulled the chain and the watch was on the other end".

"My client has a dozen witnesses who are prepared to back up his claim that he was in the cafe for two hours before you went there, and that he did not leave at any time".

"They're all liars".

"Are you saying Officer, that my client has conspired with his witnesses, to commit perjury if necessary?"

"I'm saying that Sir, yes".

"Do you realise how serious such an accusation is?"

"Do you realise what a serious accusation you are making against me, Sir?"

"I have put a question to you Officer. It is not for you to query my submission or to accuse my client or his witnesses. My client has implied that you planted that watch on him and I am calling upon you to answer that allegation".

At this point the Magistrate interjected.

"Mr. Bell", he said. "I don't think we need to go into any kind of a slanging match in Court. The solicitor for the defence has put a point and is requiring you to answer it. Do you deny the allegations put to you?"

"I deny it most strongly Sir. I am an honest Police Officer. My job is to enforce the law in a lawful manner. I am on oath and I respect that oath. I have been accused of perjury and of planting that watch on the accused. My character has been put on trial. I think, your worships, that you should, at this stage, look at the accused's previous convictions".

The defence solicitor object strongly at this suggestion.

"Your worships", he retorted. "This practice is most unorthodox. This Officer is suggesting that you study my client's previous character at a stage in proceedings which makes such a move most undesirable".

"The Officer's character has been brought into questions", said the Magistrate. "I think Mr. Bell is entitled to prove his point; and I hope that you can back up your accusations against this Detective, or be prepared to call good and convincing evidence to back up your allegations".

The solicitor looked pale and nervous. He had overplayed his game. The Magistrate leaned over and spoke to the clerk.

"Have you the accused's antecedence there?", he asked. The clerk hand him a sheet of paper. The Magistrate read in silence, his eyebrows rising suddenly. He peered at the accused over the top of his glasses. "It says here", he began, addressing the defence solicitor, "that your client has been convicted of Perjury, two years ago, and of conspiracy to pervert the course of justice, three months later. He went to a Detention Centre for those offenses. What have you to say about that?", he said, and a deep frown set across his ageing brow. Bell stood in the witness box, watching the reactions of the solicitor and of Parks.

"Your worships", began the solicitor, "I had no idea that my client had such previous convictions. He assured me that his only previous convictions were for theft. I must admit, I did not make enquiries of the Police as to his previous character".

"And have you any record of such previous findings against this Police Officer?", the Magistrate said, pointedly glaring at the defence solicitor.

"No your worship, of course not".

"Very well then", said the Magistrate. "I think you have something to say to Mr. Bell - publicly".

The solicitor fumbled with his papers, dropped them on the bench, and nervously brushed his hair back with the flat of his hand. He looked around the crowded Court, then at Bell, who remained serious and steadfast.

"Mr. Bell", the solicitor began. "I apologise for the accusation I made. I withdraw my remarks. I have no desire to discredit you or the work you do as a Police Officer". He turned to the Magistrate. "Your worship, I have no further questions to put to this Officer".

"Thank you", said the Magistrate. "You may step down Officer".

The Magistrate once more addressed the defence solicitor. "Do you wish to call witnesses for your client now?"

The solicitor had words with Parks and there was much shaking of heads.

"Your worships, my client has decided against calling witnesses", he said.

"Very well", replied the Magistrate. "Then in that case, we find there is a case to answer. The accused will be committed in custody to stand his trial at the next Crown Court. Have you an application to make on his behalf Mr. Rodgers?"

The defence solicitor stood. "Yes Sir", he replied. "I apply for a Defence Certificate on behalf of my client. He is unemployed and has no means of financial backing".

"Very well", said the Magistrate, "a defence certificate is granted".

"I am obliged your worship", said Rodgers, and he turned and picked up his papers, and stuffed them into his shiny briefcase. The escort took Bimbo Parks down to the cells under protest.

"I want to make a complaint against that bastard Bell. He assaulted me!" - but the complaint fell upon deaf ears.

The solicitor hurried out of Court, too embarrassed to face Bell or any of the Court officials. The press, he knew, would make a big splash out of the hearing. What a fool he had been, he thought, to lift reporting restrictions.

"Well done, Harry", said Bill Peterson who had been standing at the back of the Court. "You put him right in his place".

"I hate bent defences", said Bell. "Most of all when they try to ruin a good copper just to save a bloody toe-rag like Bimbo Parks".

The evening papers reported well, in spite of certain restrictions concerning the previous convictions of the accused. Nevertheless, a full and lurid report of the solicitor's apology in open court, was published and the right noises were made in the right places as a result.

Chapter 16

Bell left the Court and looked at his watch as he went out through the big swing doors. Behind him, a crowd of leather jacketed youths were chuntering in the Court foyer. He lit a cigarette.
"Twelve thirty, time for a pint, I bloody need one", Bell said to himself. He called to Peterson who was just leaving the Court.
"Coming over the Badger, Bill - I'll buy you a pint".

Peterson hurried to his side. "Certainly", he said, "you can buy me a pint any time, Harry".

They went to the 'Badger' across the road, and ordered two pints of bitter. Bell drank thirstily and the barmaid quipped about his thirst. He felt better after the second pint and decided it was time for something to eat. The canteen meal was, as usual, plain, but nourishing and it was cheap enough. Bell ate in silence.

That afternoon he walked down town. The sun was shining and the town was crowded. He walked through the shoppers and the crowds and enjoyed the open air. The noises of the traffic and the babbling of people in conversation, provided a semi-musical background to the urban scene. A short, curly haired Scotsman carrying a sandwich board, glided along in the gutter, advertising the forthcoming films at the A.B.C. Cinema. As he moved, he called in his deep, rasping voice, "Valley of the Dolls - All next week", and his right arm waved the traffic by as if he were driving a car. He came to a junction and gave a perfect left turn signal and did a smart left turn on the spot, like a guardsman on the parade ground. He was a familiar figure about the town, and people were always fascinated by his deep, throaty voice and his precise hand signals.

Bell turned the corner and came face to face with two drunks in stand-up combat. They wrestled and swore and staggered drunkenly against a shop window which bent and gave way beneath their weight. The glass shattered and the two drunks fell in and landed amongst cream cakes, pastries and broken glass, amid screams and shouts from within. One of the drunks had cut his hand, and the blood turned the cream into a strawberry red. A crowd gathered.

Harry Bell pushed his way through the crowd and grabbed both drunks by their collars. They were shocked and mumbling incoherently. He stood them up on the pavement. "Come on you two", he said. "You're both under arrest - Drunk and disorderly and causing criminal damage to that window". He took them into the shop and the manageress shrank back.

"Where's your office?", Bell said.

"In there", the manageress said, pointing to a door at the rear.

"Good - I'm a Police Officer", he went on "can I hold these two in there until the uniform lads arrive with transport?"

"Oh, yes - of course Officer", the woman said, hesitantly.

"There is a telephone in there too, if you want to use it".

"Fine", replied Bell, and he dragged his two charges into the office and shut the door.

He threw them down onto the floor and grabbed a silk scarf from around the scrawny neck of the one who was bleeding. He wrapped it haphazardly around the bleeding hand and told them both to shut up. He picked up the receiver and dialled the Police Station. Transport was ordered and two uniformed Officers despatched to take over.

"Who the 'ell are you then mate?", one of the drunks muttered.

"Shut up", demanded Bell.

"Hey!", said the other drunk. "I'll belt you, mate. We're getting out of here".

"Sit down", ordered Bell. "Or I'll do the bloody belting, you drunken slobs; now sit there and shut up or I'll put my boot right in your drunken mouths".

"Are you bleedin' C.I.D., mate?", the first one said.

"That's right", said Bell, "so shut up".

There was a clatter outside and the door opened. Two big uniformed Constables came in.

"Hello Harry", the first one said. "What's the trouble?"

"Just a couple of drunks. Fighting in the street. Fell through the plate glass window and smashed it all over the cakes. I happened to be passing and saw it all, and nicked 'em. Haven't got any statements or anything, you'll have to get them later. I'll make one when I get back to the nick".

"Okay Harry", said the Officer. "Leave them to us, we'll sort them out".

"Cheers Charlie", said Bell, "I'm obliged to you".

The two Constables picked up the drunks roughly, marched them unceremoniously out through the crowded shop and threw them into the back of the Transit van, windows barred. The van drove off up the road, and Bell had words with the shaking manageress. Two assistants were busy cleaning out the messy window display.

"Thank you very much Officer", the manageress said. "I'm very glad you were outside when it happened, I wouldn't have known what to do".

"Any time", said Bell, smiling; and he walked away.

Chapter 17

The Transit van arrived a few minutes later at the Police Station, and the Constables dragged their drunken prisoners out by the scruffs of their dirty necks. They were both itinerants with no fixed abodes. One had half a bottle of meths tucked into his pocket. The other smelt strongly of cheap wine. They were on the road and had travelled over half the country together. Occasionally they fought over trivialities, as they had today.

Charlie, the older of the two Policemen, ran his hands over the drunks, professionally. He searched their pockets and withdrew from one's old raincoat pocket, a hard, stale, mouldy, blue, curly crust of bread which must have been a month old. He threw it down on to the charge room table and it fell with a loud thump.

"Christ Almighty!", he exclaimed with disgust. "You don't want that, do you?"

"No", said the drunk, staggering and eyeing up the piece of offensive bread, "I'll 'ave it in the mornin'".

"Come on then", said the younger policeman, having completed what he could of the charge sheets. "Let's have you down here. You can sleep it off and see the Magistrates in the morning. I'll charge you both when you're sober".

The drunks were escorted to the cells where they were bedded down without mattresses or blankets - in case of accidents. Their shoes were removed at arms length and the foul stench of unwashed feet filled the cells immediately. The Constables withdrew quickly, kicking the offending shoes out through the open doors before them. They clanged the heavy metal doors and gasped for fresh air.

"By the bloody centre", exclaimed the younger Constable "Phew, what a bloody state to be in". He laughed at the sudden thought that struck him. "I hope no one goes in there and lights a bloody match", he said. "The place will go up like a bleedin' gas cylinder".

Charlie chuckled. "Some people", he said, "just don't know how to live a decent life; still, I suppose they're happy in their own way".

What did you have to go and bring those smelly bastards in for?", the Station Inspector queried. "Couldn't you have dealt with them by process, or better still, dump them over the County boundary?"

"Sorry Sir", said Charlie. "Harry Bell had already arrested them when we arrived".

"Typical - bloody typical", growled the Inspector, a man with thirty two years' service and no longer keen to have a lot of work on his hands; "Typical bloody C.I.D."

Charlie grinned. "Well, they have got a detected criminal damage out of it, Sir".

"Bah!", said the Inspector, and he stalked off to his office mumbling obscenities about the plain clothes branch.

Chapter 18

Harry Bell turned into Bourne Hill and walked to number twenty-five. He stepped gingerly down the concrete, weed covered steps leading to the basement door, and knocked. There was no reply. He opened the door and stepped into the main room. A group of five leather jacketed youths, the White Cow crowd, were lounging about the room. Penny was lying on the bed, naked. Two youths were holding her hands outstretched, and another was having intercourse with her. She was sobbing, but didn't seem to know what was happening. The youths were all counting as the fifth one plunged himself into her. Each time he moved inwards, the count increased until finally, "Fifty", and the youth withdrew and stood up, beaming as he tucked his spurting penis into his greasy jeans and zipped up the flies. A cheer went up and they all patted him on the back. "Good for you Bog", the leader said, "you lasted longer than any of us".

Bell was sickened by the sight. It was quite obvious that all five had raped the girl, now lying helpless and bleeding on the bed, her thighs wet and greasy. She was groaning and her head rolling loosely. The leader of the gang turned and saw Bell standing inside the door.

"Hey man, you come too late for your turn, we've finished the bang session", he laughed and his mates joined him, jeering and laughing at the shocked Detective.

"You're an evil shower of bastards", said Bell softly. "How can you claim membership to the human race. You're just bloody animals".

"Now watch it Daddyoh", said the leader. "How can you say that; you're just a bleedin' Pig yourself".

He pushed Bell on the shoulder and half spun him round. Bell stood firm and approached the girl.

"Leave 'er alone, Fuzz", said the leader, "she's alright, just a bit shagged for the minute", and he laughed and all the others laughed again with him.

Bell looked at them and turned his lip up in a sneer. He couldn't stand such ignorant yet arrogant people; absolutely depraved and lacking in any form of respect or regard for humanity. They had defiled this young girl unmercifully and they were laughing about it even in the face of the law. He made his move and grabbed the youth whom he had seen raping the girl, and spun him round to face him.

"I'm arresting you for a start", he said, "for rape". He glared at the others. "And in due course, I'm going to put everyone of you away for rape and administering drugs to this girl for the purpose of having intercourse. I'll have the lot of you, just you see".

The leader turned on him. "You fink we're gonna let you take 'im off to yer bloody nick, you got another fink comin' mate". He stepped forward and struck Bell across the face with his beringed hand, causing blood to seep from a newly made gash in Bell's cheek. "Take that you bleedin' Pig", he said, "and that".

He laid his boot into Bell's shin and sent him sprawling on the greasy carpet. They all crowded around him and put their boots into his body, ribs, groin, head and arms. Bell curled up as best he could, to protect his vital parts, and he felt the boots hammering into him. Then, as the pain increased, the bootings stopped and he heard footsteps running out of the house and up the slippery steps. Glass shattered as a boot came through the window, covering him with sharp slivers. He lay there, unable to move, then unconsciousness took over and he passed out.

Chapter 19

Bell came round eventually and was aware of bright lights in the room, and of hands slapping at his face. Voices sounded a long way off and his eyes ached terribly. He tried to open them, but the harshness of the arc lights blinded him and he closed them again quickly. He tried to lift himself up but found that his back ached so much that he dropped back onto the floor.

He opened his eyes again, a little at a time, and saw Detective Chief Inspector Frost, kneeling beside him. Detective Inspector Summers was also in the room, as was Bill Peterson and the Scenes of Crime Officer. Even the County Detective Superintendent was there, and there was much activity in the room, particularly around the bed.

"He's coming round", he heard a voice say, and he recognised the voice of his governor, Frost."Take it easy now", the voice went on. He felt helping hands around his shoulders and his back supported by someone from behind. He sat up on the floor and heaved as if to be sick. He felt himself shaking.

"Must be shock", he thought to himself. He saw blood on his suit and as he lifted his hand to his face, he felt the roughness of the blood where it had congealed around the wound on his cheek.

Gradually, he became aware of the situation and made an effort to stand.

"Easy now Harry", said Frost, helping him to his feet and over to a chair. Bell looked towards the bed. He could see through the crowd, the frail body of young Penny Whiteman, lying there on the bed where he had last seen her before the gang had attacked him. She was perfectly still now, eyes staring at the grubby ceiling, hands clenched into tight fists, arms outstretched and legs slightly parted. He heaved, and someone brought him a bucket into which he could be sick. He let go and brought up. Who would ever have thought it? Harry Bell, veteran of many a sordid and unpleasant sight, now being sick at the sight of a murdered young girl.

Peterson lit a cigarette and put it into Harry's mouth. He sucked hard, inhaled the thick smoke and closed his eyes.

"Alright Bell" - it was the Detective Superintendent speaking. "It's time we heard from you. You have a lot to tell us".

Bell looked up into the cold, hard eyes of the Superintendent. He was a good Detective and had much experience in the ground work, unlike so many of the breed of Senior Officers, the high flyers who went from recruit to the top of the ladder in ten to fifteen years. No, Gray had worked his way to the top, the hard way, and he knew the job inside out. Bell respected Superintendent Gray.

"What's happening - what's going on?", asked Bell at last, confused and bemused.

"Don't you know?", asked Gray.

"No, not really", said Bell. "Unless - yes, that's it.....", he paused as if trying to remember something.

"Well, what is it Bell?", said Frost, impatiently. The Superintendent interjected.

"Bell", he said. "A young girl has been murdered. At least she's dead, and she appears to have been savagely raped. Someone telephoned the police - an anonymous caller, telling us to get here as soon as we could. They didn't say why. One of the uniformed cars came here to investigate and the driver found you and that girl. They sent for us straight away. We've been here about half an hour".

"Have I been out all that time Sir?", Bell asked, surprised.

"Yes", said Gray. "The Police Surgeon was here and he didn't see the need for an ambulance to get you to hospital, but I think you had better go anyway, for a check up".

"Thank the Police Surgeon for me Sir", said Bell, sarcastically.

"Well, can you tell me what happened Bell?".

"I came here this afternoon Sir, about five o'clock I suppose. I wanted to see Penny Whiteman".

"What for?"

"I found her suffering from withdrawal symptoms the other day and got her to hospital. She told me something about her pusher and things. Agreed to go into a clinic for a cure. Then I found out a few days later, that she had discharged herself. I came her to see if she was alright and try to get her to get treatment for her drug addiction".

"You know who her pusher was?"

"Yes".

"Who?"

"Chap called Roger Bender".

"Do we know him?"

"Yes Sir, he's on record".

"Make a note of that, Frost - we'll have to interview him. He's a good suspect for a start". He turned back to Bell.

"What else then Bell. What happened when you got here today?"

"I arrived here and knocked on the door. No one answered and I heard these voices inside. I opened the door and came in. There was a gang of yobs in leather jackets inside, you know the types, all chains and brass studs and long dirty hair. Well, they were all standing around. Two were holding Penny's arms out and another was having intercourse with her. They were all counting each time he penetrated. They counted fifty and he got off. He was still ejaculating as he stood up. They said something about a banging session, then they saw me. I tried to arrest the one I had seen at it, but they all attacked me and put the boot in. I don't know any more".

"So that was it", said Gray. "A gang-bang". He stood up and looked down at Bell. "The bastards. Do you think you'll recognise them again, Bell?"

"Oh yes Sir, I'll bloody recognise them. They're the White Cow cafe bunch".

"Names?"

"Sorry Sir, can't give you any names. I nicked two of them the other day though - Bimbo Parks and Bernard Smedley. They may be able to put us on to the names of the other yobs in the gang".

"Was Smedley or Parks there today?"

"No Sir, Parks is inside - Smedley, well I don't know where he is, but he lives locally".

"Good man, Bell", said Gray. "We should get somewhere with this one, I think".

Frost looked at Bell, then at Gray. "I think we ought to get Bell to hospital Sir, for a check up, don't you?"

"Yes Mr. Frost. I think we had better do that. Get someone to take him, will you? I'll see you later Bell and get a statement from you when you've had time to think a little more about it - alright?"

"Alright Sir, thank you", said Bell.

Peterson drove Bell to the General Hospital where he was seen by the Duty Casualty Officer and treated. He was allowed to go home after a night's observation. He had been concussed and they liked to keep patients in overnight in such circumstances.

Chapter 20

After spending the night in hospital, Harry Bell was released feeling a little sore and still rather tired. Nevertheless, he wanted to get back to duty. He had a score to settle with the milk bar crowd, and he wanted to waste no time about it.

He walked into the incident room which had been set up at the local Police Station. The recreation room had been converted temporarily, into a hive of activity. Officers of varying rank, sat around a large central table, typing, reading statements and indexing material points. A Detective Sergeant scribbled out 'Action' slips detailing Officers of the appointed Murder Squad, for routine jobs, statement taking, checking alibis and making enquiries at relevant quarters. The Superintendent was in conference with the Assistant Chief Constable and the other heads of C.I.D.

"What's doing then Serge?", Bell asked the Detective Sergeant in front of whom was a notice printed in large, black stencil, 'Action Man'.

"Hello Harry", replied the Sergeant, surprise showing in his tone. "Didn't expect to see you in today. How are you?"

"I'm pretty sore and full of aches and pains, but otherwise I'll live", said Bell. "Am I on the team?"

The Detective Sergeant looked at his colleague. "I don't know Harry", he said. "You'll have to see Mr. Gray - he is doing the appointing".

"Well, I'm bloody well on, whether he likes it or not", said Bell militantly. "Christ, I'm the major bloody witness".

"Well, you know how it is Harry - anyway, see him after his conference. He should be finished soon".

Bell picked up the message book and began to read the information. He briefed himself as to what had taken place to date, and sifted through the papers looking for a hint of anything that would tell him exactly how far they had got.

The door opened and Superintendent Gray came rushing in, followed by a Detective Inspector drafted in from Headquarters for the occasion, mainly to help swell the numbers rather than for his value as a Detective.

"I don't care how long it will take", Gray was saying loudly and with authority: "get it done. I want all those records up from the yard and then I want all the files we have at headquarters on rapes and indecency over the past two years. Don't tell me it's a big job - I know it is - but don't let it worry you Smith, just keep at it and you'll come to the end eventually".

Smith, a pale weedy looking man who rarely saw the sunshine, bowed his head sulkily. He fumbled for words then decided against replying.

"You can take that side kick of yours from H.Q. C.I.D. He knows as much about the records as you do Smith - right off you go".

Smith disappeared with his tail between his legs and Gray picked up the latest bulletin and read. He finished and dropped the bulletin on the 'Action Man's' desk, then looked up and saw Bell standing in the corner.

"Ah! D.C. Bell", he declared. "Glad to see you up and about. Are you feeling alright now then? Feeling up to it today are we?" He smiled.

"Yes Sir, I think so", said Bell, trying to muster a smile. "I'm ready to go to work Sir, if you want me on the team".

"What a man! 'course we want you on the team. Wouldn't do without you. Now then, I think you had better come through to my office and we'll have a talk about this thing. I want your story and I want to get it into writing. The Chief Constable is getting impatient and has been on to me for your statement. I've had to put him off of course, but he'll be wanting it today, that's for sure".

Bell followed the man into an adjoining office and sat down in a large comfortable, leather-bound chair. He accepted a cigarette which the Superintendent lit for him. Bell pressed his free hand against his bruised ribs and made a face.

"Hurt still, does it, Harry?", the Superintendent said. Bell nodded. He appreciated the Superintendent's respect for his Detectives and knew that when the Super called you by your christian name, he thought something of you.

"Do you know the cause of death yet Sir?", Bell queried.

"Yes", replied Gray. "Pathologist's report came in at nine o'clock this morning. She died primarily of shock, accelerated by the overall effects of constant use of heroin. Her death however, was directly attributed to the shock brought on by the repeated raping and ill-treatment by those bastards who also had a go at you". He paused and sighed. "She also lost a lot of blood - internally. I can't understand such animals, I really can't".

Bell was silent. He felt a little sick again. The words he had spoken to Penny had been wasted. He had thought that his advice had sunk in and he expected that she would do as he suggested and accept help and treatment. Had she done so, she would never have become the victim of these beasts. "This bloody town", he thought, "is a jungle. It is a vicious and evil town, where human beings are secondary to money and lust. Where self destruction and degradation lurks around every corner, waiting to impose itself upon the next innocent intruder. It is a cesspit, where, it seems, to ferment and rot and infect everyone and everything it comes into contact with. A human garbage heap, where a human being is nothing but an object to be moved in furtherance of self-gratification". Bell thought on in silence and then realised that Gray was looking at him as if expecting an answer.

"You alright Bell?", Gray asked.

"Oh sorry Sir", snapped Bell. "I was caught up in thought".

"You looked pretty bitter right then".

"Yes Sir - I feel that way".

"Well come on then, let's get on with the job in hand. Now then, can you remember any more than you told us last night?"

Bell thought for a moment. His thoughts had in fact been on the subject for hours.

"I heard a name Sir", he said. "The one I actually saw raping the girl. They called him 'Bog', like the shit-house he really is. That's the only name I heard Sir. The one who seemed to be their leader was a tall, thin object with long black, greasy hair below his shoulders. He wore a black leather jacket with swastika's all over the place, chains and brass studs and things. Oh, and he wore a badge on his left sleeve, with a picture of a Red Indian chief on it. He needed a shave. I'll recognise him again without any doubt at all, and the one they called Bog. The rest of them, I can identify and describe Sir".

"Good for you Bell", Gray said, eagerly. "Let's start right at the beginning then, from the time you first went to the place and found the girl in the toilet. Take it from there, everything you can tell me".

Bell spent a considerable time with Gray, detailing everything he could come up with concerning Penny and her associates. HE even mentioned the parties she had told him about, and the people she mentioned.

It was one fifteen that afternoon before Bell was through with his statement. He had exhausted his knowledge on the subject and it was all in writing. His evidence would, without a doubt, clear up the case. He was lucky to be in the position to finger the culprits in such a terrible crime. The Superintendent was well pleased and Bell knew that this was just the kind of thing that would bring his name to the Chief Constable's attention and when that happens, who knows how far away promotion would be?

Gray took Bell to lunch. They didn't eat in the Station canteen, instead they went to the new 'Thistledown Hotel', where the food was expensive and good. Bell dined well that day and rounded off his meal with a brandy, all on the Superintendent's expense account. Bell hoped, all through the meal, that Ruby would not show up, this being one of her favourite haunts. He would rather that Gray knew nothing of his association with her, and he didn't want to involve her unnecessarily in this case. She didn't show.

It didn't take long to round up the whole crowd from the White Cow cafe. A dozen Detectives accompanied by an equal number of their uniformed colleagues, raided the place that evening when it was packed to capacity. Twenty three leather jacketed, long haired youths were picked up and taken unceremoniously to the Police Station under extreme protest.

"Out - the lot of you", barked a big uniformed Sergeant in the station yard. "And bloody move your idle selves - what did you say sonny?" He glared at a stocky youth with too much chewing gum in his mouth, big though it was; and a Nazi iron cross around his neck. "You got something to say to me, say it so I can hear. Now, what you got to say lad?"

"Nuffink mate", the youth spat.

The Sergeant grabbed the unfortunate youth by the hair and dragged him out of the van. "Nothing what?", the Sergeant roared.

"Nothing Sergeant", replied the youth, cowering a little and blushing all over.

"That's bloody right", said the Sergeant. "Nothing Sergeant. If you don't want to call me Sergeant, call me Sir!, and stand up straight when you talk to me; do I make myself clear, you slimy little slob?"

"Yes Sir", said the youth, straightening a little.

"Right then, and that goes for the lot of you".

The ragged file of youths were led inside and lined up in the charge room passage. An Inspector came in with a clip board and took each of their names and addresses, dates of birth and height. Having completed the list, he removed the carbon copy and handed it to a Detective who was at his arm.

"Here we are then Fred", he said; "get that lot checked out with the Yard and see if any of 'em are wanted. This is a good chance to check them all out". The Detective made off and soon the teleprinter was chattering its list of names to Scotland Yard, Criminal Records Office.

After considerable messing about and delay, Harry Bell was brought in and stood at the beginning of the ragged line.

"If you see any of the youths you recognise as having been present at number twenty five Bourne Hill yesterday afternoon, will you please tap him on the shoulder and say nothing". The Inspector instructed Bell then stood back and half a dozen Constables and a couple of Detectives watched silently from the end of the passage.

Bell walked along the line slowly, looking into the faces of each in turn. He came to Bernard Smedley and stopped. He stared at him, knowing that he was not one of the culprits, but determined to give him a bit of a sweat just the same. He just stared hard at

Smedley and grinned inwardly as he saw the beads of perspiration start to form on the youth's forehead. The face became a deathly grey and nerves turned his languid body into a shivering mould. Bell walked on and stopped three down. He had no doubt at all. He put his hand firmly on the shoulder of the one called 'Bog'. The youth, a wiry youngster of about seventeen, passed out and lay on the concrete floor. Bell walked another five paces and stopped again. He recognised the scar across the cheek of the red-headed, evil looking youth wearing this hair down to his collar, and with a blue stoned brooch pinned to his jacket above a German S.S. Colonel's emblem. He had been one of the two holding Penny's arms. Bell put his hand on the youth's shoulder and the Inspector made due note of it. Bell still continued along the line and picked two more then completed his walk. The fifth one didn't appear to be there. He walked back again along the line to the start but the leader of the gang was missing.

The identification parade was over and Bell left the passage. He stood by Superintendent Gray.

"What about the fifth one then Harry?", Gray asked. "Isn't he there then?"

"No Sir, he definitely isn't there. He must have gone to ground".

"Alright", said Gray, "we'll make a start with these. You're pretty sure about these I hope?"

"No doubt at all Sir", said Bell. "That's them alright".

"Right".

The Detective with the list of names came back and handed it to the Superintendent. Five of the men in the line were wanted by other forces for various offenses, and one was on the run from a Borstal on the South Coast. All in all, a good day's work. Fourteen youths left the Police Station, somewhat subdued and feeling rather silly.

"What about the leader fellow then Harry?", Gray said as they passed in the canteen later. "Do you know where he can be picked up?"

"I've no doubt we can manager that without too much bother Sir", said Bell. "I'll get on to it myself, we should get a lead somewhere".

The four suspects for the murder were taken away and placed in separate cells. They were left to sweat for half an hour before anyone came to see them at all. Finally Gray went into the cell where Bog was lying on the wooden bed.

"On your feet lad", he said. "Name?"

"Walter French Sir", the youth quivered.

"How old are you?"

"Seventeen"

"Parents?"

"They've cleared off. I'm on me own".

"What's the name of the leader of your little lot. The one who was with you in the flat but who isn't here today?? He's going to let you lot take the rap for him isn't he? You admire him do you - coward enough to clear off and leave you lot to take it all yourselves. Well, what's his name then?"

"Lance Rodway, Sir", the trembling lad said.

"Where is he?"

"Dunno".

Gray called to the gaoler. "Tell D.C. Bell that the leader's name is Lance Rodway".

"Right Sir", said the gaoler, and he hurried away.

"Now then lad", continued Gray. "What about this gang-bang then, eh? You're going to tell me about it aren't you?"

"Look Guv'nor, I don't know nuffink about it, see".

"You were there", Gray said. "weren't you?"

"Well, no, not exactly".

"You said you were there just now. You told me the name of Rodway. You didn't deny that you were there then, did you?"

"Alright, I was there; but it wasn't like you think".

"You know why you are here lad, don't you? You have been arrested for rape. The girl is dead - did you know that you killed her, French?"

"Dead".....Whotcher mean Guv'nor. I didn't kill her".

"You raped her didn't you?"

"Well, yes....kind of - but she didn't resist".

"Was she in any condition to resist?"

"Well, she just sort of laid there".

"Yes, and all five of you raped her, didn't you?"

"Alright, I'll admit that much, but we didn't murder her".

"Good", said Gray. "Now we have got this far, I think I had better caution you that you need not say anything more unless you wish to do so but whatever you do say, will be put into writing and may be given in evidence. Is that clear?"

"Yes Sir".

"Right then, now that's out of the way, tell me all about it".

French related the whole story, how the gang had been on the rampage, and how Rodway had suggested getting hold of a girl, any girl, for a gang-bang. They had wandered about, then Rodway had said that he knew a girl, Penny something or other, who would be easy meat. He had led them to twenty five Bourne Hill where they had burst in on the unsuspecting Penny. They had thrown her on to the bed amid protests, and stripped her, then one by one, raped her unmercifully. She stopped struggling after the second one had had it. And so the sordid story unrolled itself in full.

Gray was pleased with the interview and, armed with a complete confession in writing under caution, he had interviewed the rest and they had all coughed. Now it remained only for the leader, Lance Rodway to be detained and charged with them. Bell was already out looking for him with several other Detectives.

Chapter 21

Reg Tomlinson, driver for Ocean Import Services Limited, slipped into the public telephone kiosk outside the main gate of the depot. He dialled a number and waited. A voice came onto the line.

"'ello", it said.

"Don?"

"Yeah".

"Reg 'ere. Got news for yer".

"Go on then, what's the score?"

"Delivery due in two days time. We've got the stuff in now and I'll be doing the drop to Quality Sound. I'll see you tonight and talk about it, okay?"

"Right", said Don Broadman. "See you".

Broadman rubbed his hands together. "Now", he thought, "I am going to get rich. This is the way to do it - easy". He grinned to himself and lit a cigarette. He dialled a number and waited. A voice on the other end sounded impatient.

"Broadman here Guv", he said. "Got a load coming up in a couple of days. How about that run-in you spoke of. I will want to have a look at it and see the layout if we're going to do the job right".

"Alright", said the voice. "See me this afternoon at Frankies cafe out on the A6 road. I'll take you there then and you can see the set-up".

"Fine", said Broadman. "Two o'clock okay?"

"Suits me", said the voice. "Be on your own".

"Will do", said Broadman, and the receiver went dead.

The Shipway Import and Export Company's warehouse at Tilbury docks, was well stocked and the latest load of radio, television and tape recording equipment was being checked in as it came off the 'Yoko Maru', a smart looking freighter registered in Tokyo. The gear looked good and was soundly packed.

Frank Weymes held his clip board and checked off the list as the stock came off the fork lift trucks. He smiled and warmed inwardly in the knowledge that this particular load was going to make him rich. He was only a stock checker, but the position gave him the opportunity to assess the best loads to be fiddled. He had got the job by special arrangement with William Chandler who had pulled strings with the management who owed him a favour. The firm itself was quite legitimate. Chandler, as he had intimated to Bell on their first meeting, had many and varied interests.....this was no exaggeration.

The stock was checked in and stored and awaited the next step. - thė delivery instructions. By the following morning, the delivery list was ready and Weymes stood on the loading bay as the equipment was being loaded into a large box truck by the loading team. Officially, the driver of the truck had not been allocated yet, but that was no problem for Weymes: after all, he handed the keys out as he thought fit and saw no problem there.

Colour television sets went in first and filled the first half of the truck. Next, the tape recording gear and finally the radio equipment. The loading took best part of the day since the work team was small and not in the least energetic. There was no hurry.

Don Broadman had arranged to have the next day off to attend his great-uncle's funeral. The excuse was in fact real, and his great-uncle was to be buried on the afternoon. He boasted that he expected to come into some money from his great-uncle's estate, albeit that his great-uncle was penniless and lived in a council flat in Buckinghamshire. However, it was a good cover for the job to be done on the morrow. His plan was to carry out his scheme in collusion with the driver, Reg Tomlinson, then, on completion, travel on to his relatives in Buckinghamshire after lunch, in time for the funeral. He would have plenty of witnesses to say that he was there, in case of any unforeseen emergency.

The loading completed, Weymes ticked off his check list then locked and sealed the vehicle before returning to the office. He marked the load up for delivery early the following morning. Having made the arrangements, he sought out Reg Tomlinson and tipped him to be at the depot at seven thirty sharp the following morning to ensure that he was available to take out the load. Weymes would make sure that they keys to the appropriate vehicle were the first on the list and therefore, Tomlinson should be first in line.

Weymes spoke to the Despatch Manager and told him that the load for Quality Sound Services was all ready and could be despatched early in the morning. The Manager was pleased. Quality Sound had been pestering him for a couple of weeks for the delivery which he had necessarily had to delay due to the ship being held up in Capetown. He was pleased to telephone Quality Sound and advise that delivery would arrive in the morning.

Chapter 22

Harry Bell was feeling rather tired and worn out. He had had a long and tedious day visiting cafes and public houses and amusement arcades in his search for Lance Rodway. In addition, he had Susan on his troubled mind and then there was the warehouse aspect of his job; a thorn in his already aching side. He was feeling like packing in for the day, providing he could persuade Gray that he had done his fair share. He turned another corner off the main road and bumped into Jimmy Bunce.

"Hello there Jimmy", he said, tiredly. "What's new then?"

"Nuffin much Guv'", Bunce sniffed. He looked as though he had been crying.

"Something wrong Jimmy?", asked Bell, offering the lad a cigarette.

"Aw - just can't get over Penny being dead, you know like - it just don't seem true".

"It's true enough Jimmy", said Bell, sympathetically. "I'm sorry".

"The word is out you want Lance Rodway", Bunce said. "That true?"

"Yes", replied Bell. "You know where I can find him?"

"Fink so, Mr. Bell. Rumour has it, he's hiding up in an old shack down at Burnham Beeches. A crowd of his cronies went there last summer for a week and made it their camp, kind of fing. They say he's got a gun now too".

"Where is this place Jimmy. Do you know?"

"No Guv'. Only know it's somewhere down Burnham Beeches. Ain't that kind of a beauty spot somewhere?"

"Yes, down in Bucks, not far from Slough, I think".

"Well, that's all I know Mr. Bell, for what it's worth".

"Thanks Jimmy. Don't worry, we'll get the bastard who did your Penny in".

Bell walked back to the Police Station and sought out Superintendent Gray. He was still in his office sifting through a pile of statements and information. Bell knocked on his door.

"Enter", came the reply.

Bell opened the door and walked in. Gray looked up and smiled.

"Come in Bell", he said, waving towards the big chair. "Sit down, won't be a moment".

Gray was silent and looked pensive. He drummed the table top with his fingers and pursed his lips.

"Where did your information come from - was it a reliable source?"

"No secret there Sir. It was Jimmy Bunce, you remember, Penny's boyfriend. Says it's the general rumour. Apparently, he believes that Rodway and his gang went there last summer for a couple of weeks".

"So we should be able to get the location from any of those bastards we have inside".

"I reckon so Sir".

"Right, come on then Bell. No time like the present, let's go up to the prison and see them shall we?"

Without any more ado, Gray stood up and nodded to Bell. Together they walked out of the door.

"I'm going to Bedford Prison", Gray called to the Detective Sergeant in charge of the incident room. And he departed with Bell in tow.

Walter French, alias Bog, was very helpful and told them, with the aid of an ordinance survey map, exactly how they could find the old woodman's shack in the woods. He had no reason to protect Rodway; after all, wasn't it Rodway who had got them into this mess in the first place? He told all he knew.

"What about the gun he's supposed to have?", asked Gray. "Is he likely to use it?"

"Wouldn't be surprised", answered the youth. "He's had it a long time. I've seen him carrying it sometimes but I don't know if he had any ammunition".

"Well, we'll be prepared for him", said Gray.

They waited until the following morning and at seven o'clock, a small convoy of three plain cars containing Detectives and one or two uniformed marksmen, left the town Police Station en-route for Burnham Beeches. Gray would not allow Bell to carry a firearm; felt he might be too ready to use it in the circumstances - emotional involvement and all that. Two Detective Sergeants and himself carried .38 revolvers and the uniformed Constables carried special marksman's rifles.

As they travelled, Bell relaxed in the back of the car alongside Superintendent Gray. He closed his eyes and allowed his mind to return to last night when he had telephoned Susan in an attempt to smooth over the bubbling volcano which seemed to be working up between them. He wanted to have her back with him but was frightened to bring her back to the danger of Chandler's wrath unnecessarily. He winced as he recalled her first reply when he identified himself to her on the telephone.

"I don't know that I want to talk to you Harry", she had said.

"What do you mean Susan?"

"I think you know the answer there. You don't want me Harry. What does it feel like to have your freedom at last?"

"Sue".

"Don't Sue me, you can work all the hours you want to now, can't you Harry? You can meet all the women you want to, and do just what you've always wanted to do".

"For Christ's sake Sue".

"And don't swear at me Harry. Mother was right about you. You're an uncouth good-for-nothing. I should have listened to her in the first place".

"Sue, listen to me, will you?"

"Do you realise Harry, that you have only telephoned me twice since I've been here and do you realise that has been three weeks now?"

"Susan will you shut up and let me speak", Bell had become impatient.

"I will do no such thing Harry. I think you had better communicate with me through a solicitor in future, and don't get our own solicitor, he's acting on my behalf".

"Hell, what do you mean, he's acting on your behalf. What for?"

"I'm leaving you Harry".

"Why?"

"Isn't it obvious?"

"No it bloody well isn't. Now what the hell's going on?"

"Well, you have technically deserted me by sending me away on some stupid pretext that it is too dangerous to stay at home. Well, if that's what you want Harry, that's your affair. I won't stand in your way if you want a divorce".

"Divorce! Who the hell said anything about a divorce?"

"I did Harry. I did". Susan had sounded defiant and adamant. She had obviously made up her mind. She was unreasonable.

"Your bloody mother has put all this rot into your mind, hasn't she Sue? I'm going to come down there and sort her and you out. Who the hell does she think she is anyway?"

"You'd better not come here causing trouble Harry", Sue said, nervously.

"Well, I'm bloody coming".

"Where were you last Wednesday night Harry? I phoned several times all through the night again. Where the hell were you, as if I didn't know?"

"You want to know where I was Sue. I was in bloody hospital!"

"Hospital!", she had echoed. "Harry, what for?"

"You don't really bloody care Susan, do you?", Bell had snapped.

"Harry, what were you doing in hospital?"

"What the hell does it matter?" "I can tell you this though it wasn't for injuries received in bed with any other woman". The note of sarcasm had cut into Susan's own bitchiness.

"Harry", she had started, but Bell had said enough. The phone clicked and Susan had been left holding a dead line.

Bell had gone home late and drunk a quarter of a bottle of scotch before going to bed. He had been awakened by the telephone operator at six o'clock as arranged. He had found himself still clothed in his suit. A shower and a shave and a complete change of clothing had put him on the right road to work, and now, here he was, on his way with his colleagues, to try to flush out a mad dropout from a shack in the woods. A nutter with a gun; the worst kind of situation that occasionally presents itself to a copper. Susan kept getting in the way of his concentration. He would have to watch out, and he knew it.

An official from the National Trust briefed Gray and his men as to the locations of the various woodsman's huts in the area. There were four altogether and most of them well hidden amid thick bushes and trees. The most likely was the one down by the great lake. It was furnished with a camp bed and a stove and one or two useful utensils. The others were just shelters, housing perhaps a wheelbarrow here or a rake or fire brush there.

Gray divided his men into three teams with the plan that they would approach the huts individually, each team approaching from different directions to give the best coverage. If the first was not successful, they would go onto the second and so on.

They approached the hut nearest the lake, from three sides with the lake on the fourth. Silently they crept through the bushes, using the trees as cover wherever possible. Gray beckoned to the Inspector in the second team and gradually the men closed in. All was silent. There was one solitary window in the back of the hut and this afforded a clear view to anyone within. Finally, when within a few yards of the hut, and still with no indication of anyone within, Gray gave the signal and the first team, his own, rushed at the front door and burst in. The other two teams closed, one on the back window and the other covering the front door. There was utter silence for a moment, then a Sergeant appeared and waved at his colleagues.

"All clear in here", he called, and the men relaxed.

Gray went over the contents of the hut with infinite care, paying attention to the minutest detail for any signs that someone had been using the place recently. He found nothing to indicate that

Rodway had been there. He stepped out into the broken sunlight which filtered through the beech trees and reflected off the shimmering lake.

"Alright men", he said. "Number two hut it is".

They formed up into three groups once more and began to trudge towards the second hut, perhaps half a mile away. Bell walked behind Gray who was discussing the progress of the case with a Detective Inspector. Bell didn't feel like company anyway.

The second hut, rather smaller than the first, and in a state of disrepair, appeared through the trees quite unexpectedly. The search group stopped suddenly and awaited orders. Gray gathered his men about him and outlined the approach format. Once again, they made their ways to three points covering the two sides and front, leaving the back uncovered, there being no window at the rear. This way, if he broke cover, it would have to be via the front door, then, whichever way he went, he could be seen and stopped, one way or another.

Bell was on his hands and knees, high ferns towering above him. He crept towards the front of the shack and his colleagues were following his example, spread out in a fan shape. Gray walked erect with a Detective Sergeant, and made his way towards the shack. He stopped about thirty yards away and waited. He watched for his men to signal that they were all within twenty five yards each side of him, and well covered, then he called.

"Rodway, this is the Police. Come out with your hands up high. We are armed and you are completely surrounded. There is no way of escape. If you come out with your hands up and throw away your gun so that we can see it, you will come to no harm. If you shoot however, we will shoot you. Do you understand?"

There was a long pause. Silence and tension cutting through the morning air. Even the birds had stopped their morning song as if knowing of the drama to be played out in front of them, disturbing the rural solitude which was their inheritance. Nothing; absolute silence.

"Rodway", Gray was calling again. "I am warning you. We are armed and you are surrounded. Come out now and you will not be harmed".

A shout from within made the hidden men jump unexpectedly. No one had really expected to find him here, but that shout from the hut brought them to their most alert pitch. Tension pulled at the muscles of the concealed men in the undergrowth as they waited for the next move.

"Clear off", the voice trembled and sounded frightened.

"Come out Rodway. You will not be harmed", repeated the Superintendent. A further pause followed, then a short answer.

"Balls".

Gray was not deterred. He knew that he must adopt the correct procedure as laid down in the Home Office Circular with regard to armed and besieged criminals. Here was a situation with all the pitfalls and dangers that the policy was designed to overcome, with the maximum safety to the Public, the Criminal himself, and the Police, in that order. As always, the Police was at the end of the list of considerations.

"Don't be a fool Rodway. We know you are armed and we are armed to match you. Our Officers are marksmen and will not miss. They will shoot if you force them to do so. I do not want anyone hurt and that includes you. So be sensible, lad, come on out now, whilst there is a chance for you".

A single shot rang out and the chinking of glass simultaneously accompanied the report. A small hole, surrounded by a sunburst of cracks appeared in the one window beside the door of the hut. A whining noise caused the Policemen in the trees to duck and hold themselves flat against the soft, cool earth as the bullet ricocheted through the trees. Gray dropped to his knees, then dashed for cover behind a fallen log. His Sergeant followed close on his heels and fell on top of him.

"The bastard", cursed Gray. "He's going to wind up in very serious trouble". Everyone remained still and silent. All eyes now on the window, strained and tried not to blink for fear of missing a vital movement.

"I warned you, Rodway", called Gray again. "For God's sake be sensible. Do you want to be shot yourself? Now stop playing games and come out".

"Get stuffed copper", came the reply. "I know your kind of promises. I step out of that door and get gunned down. I know your type".

"Don't be a fool Rodway. We wouldn't shoot unless we had to and that depends entirely upon your action. If you throw your gun out and come out with your hands up, you will come to no harm".

"Bollocks", came the reply, followed by another shot. Gray winced as the shell tore into the tree trunk above his head.

"Sergeant", bellowed Gray. "A shot in through that window, just a warning".

Bang! The Sergeant's revolver barked and the glass in the little window fell out completely. The bullet tore through the back wall and out into the woods beyond. There was a yell from within.

"Are you coming out now Rodway?", called the Superintendent once more.

"You'll have to come and bloody get me if you want me" replied Rodway, fear reflecting in his voice. A further shot rang out from within the shack and a uniformed Constable beside Bell jerked as the lead tore into his shoulder. Bell grabbed the man and tore his jacket off. He exposed the wound and saw that the bullet had smashed the man's shoulder bone and travelled through. He applied pressure above the wound and called to a Sergeant.

"Bailey's been hit Serge", he called. "In his shoulder".

Gray overheard the call and ordered his Sergeant to open up with two more shots through the window. The two shots rang out and echoed through the silent morning. "You have hit and wounded one of my men Rodway", Gray called, anger now beginning to show in his voice. "I do not intend to allow you to injure any more of my men. Now, if you don't come out, we will have to come in and I will not hesitate to shoot you".

"Balls", came the truculent reply, followed by more shots.

The door of the shack opened slowly, and Bell saw the barrel of a revolver pointing towards him although he was concealed himself. He saw Rodway's ugly face in the light as he came out. Rodway started to shoot in all directions and then aimed deliberately at Superintendent Gray who was now fully exposed, having come out from his cover in order to lead his men into the shack. Rodway's revolver lifted and held firm. Gray froze, his own revolver still holstered. Bell looked about him, expecting to hear a shot from one of the Police guns - but none came. He looked to his right and saw a Detective Sergeant aiming a revolver at Rodway. His arm was shaking and sweat soaked his brow.

"Shoot for Christ's sake Serge, shoot", said Bell fiercely.

"I........I can't", mumbled the Sergeant. "I just can't shoot a man".

"Well for Christ's sake", said Bell, grabbing the gun from the Sergeant, "give the bloody thing here".

Rodway was talking. "....I'll bleedin' shoot your fat head off if you move copper", he was peering at Gray, now standing perfectly still, about fifteen yards away. Bell saw the whites of Rodways, knuckles as his fist tightened on the pistol grip and he saw the trigger finger move a little more. He did not hesitate further; Bell tightened his own finger on the trigger of the Sergeant's .38 and squeezed. The barrel was pointing directly at Rodway's chest.

Boom! The Police revolver barked, and the barrel lifted as it recoiled. Rodway dropped like a stone, the pistol falling from his hands as he went down on to the soft turf. A patch of red appeared instantly from his right temple and over the fresh green grass below his shattered head.

The Superintendent stood stock still, unbelieving. Seconds passed by before there was movement from the men in concealment, and Bell stood up, gun in hand, now pointing earthwards. He felt no emotion at all.

Gray strode over to the very dead form of Rodway and peered unbelievingly down at him. He seemed to be mesmerised by the sight. He looked up and his eyes went from one Officer to the other. They finally came to rest upon Bell, gun still in his hand, face grim, unemotional, hard and purposeful.

"I thought I said you were not to be armed, Bell", he said at last.

"Yes Sir", said Bell, perhaps a little insubordinately.

"Where did you get that firearm?", Gray asked, softly.

"It's mine Sir", said the Sergeant from whom Bell had snatched the gun.

"Why has he got your gun?"

"I....I couldn't use it Sir", said the Sergeant, a little embarrassed.

Gray turned his gaze to Bell and studied the hard features. He knew that he had expected to die at any moment, at the hands of the maniac Rodway; and he realised that he had prayed for someone to pull a trigger. Then, the relief as he had heard the single shot ring out and Rodway's life had been ended. He had not intended that Rodway should be shot, of course. One never wanted to shoot, and certainly did not want to kill a wanted criminal. But then, sometimes it just had to be. This was, without a doubt, such an occasion.

Gray's eyes fixed themselves upon Bell and saw the man he had come to like and admire. Here was a man to be relied upon; he saw a hard yet honest man in Bell. A man who knew his place and his job. A man of humility and strength. His kind of man; and now he owed his life to Bell's quick appreciation of the situation, and for that he was indeed grateful. He looked at the men surrounding him and then back at Bell. "Thank you Harry", he said. "You saved my life".

Bell did not reply. He handed the gun to a Detective Inspector at his side. "You'll be wanting this Sir", he said. "The forensic people will want to examine it to compare it with the bullet in that fellow's head just to prove that it was a Police bullet that killed him. There's bound to be a hoo haa, I reckon".

He walked away into the woods and sat on a log about a hundred yards away, lit a cigarette and blew out smoke. He closed his eyes and thought about his life. What a mess he had got into during these past few weeks. Chandler had been the cause of the events that had wrecked his marriage; that had driven him into the chase for the drugs distributors; that had indirectly brought him into contact with black Ruby and caused him to be unfaithful to his wife. And now, through snowballing events that had led to the chase for Rodway, had caused him, Harry Bell, to kill in the course of his duty, a point yet to be proved in a Coroner's Court. Would the jury accept that his action was called for? or would the jury accept that there was no evidence to support that Rodway would have pulled the trigger if Bell had not dropped him when he had? The outcome of the inquest would determine the rest of Bell's career - his entire life perhaps.

Bell dwelt on these things and felt no pity, no remorse for Rodway, nor bitterness for the Sergeant who had trembled and caused Bell to do his dirty work for him. He just felt a numbness. He was tired - damned tired. Too bloody much had happened to him in too short a time. The pace of life was so fast in the environment in which he had found himself working since his transfer to the big city-like town not far from London itself. He had always fancied big-town work since he had joined the Force in one of the South Coast Provinces ten years before. He had transferred to the big town after six years and then his chance came and he was appointed to the Criminal Investigation Department. He found the work exciting and more interesting but the pace was fast.......yes, bloody fast, and he had somehow managed to keep up with it; but there comes a time, as Bell was finding out, when one cannot keep up with it any more, and things start to go wrong both at home and on the job. Bell's time seemed to have come.

"Perhaps I'll resign", he thought as they travelled back to the Station. The formalities at the scene had been dealt with, and the necessary investigation of the incident on the spot had been completed for the moment. Bell sat silently at the back of the big car and thought.

"Resignation, that's it. Susan might find it to her advantage to have me out of the job. She never did like me doing this job anyway. Yes....I'll resign, but not until I've nailed that bastard Chandler who started it all off".

"Well Harry", said Gray, breaking the long silence. "I think we've just about cleared this one now. Only remains for the Court case to be dealt with and that's the end of another one. I think you should have a spot of leave. Have you had your annual leave yet?"

"No Sir".

"Then I think you had better take it soon".

"I'd rather not have it until I've finished an enquiry I'm stuck on already Sir".

"What's that?"

"A man I'm after Sir. William Chandler he calls himself. Big time racketeer I think, a bit evasive, but I'm on to him I'm sure. I want to finish this one, then I think I'll have my leave".

"Well, it's up to you Harry. Just don't leave it too long, alright?"

"Alright Sir", said Bell, solemnly.

Chapter 23

There was an urgent message waiting for Bell when he got back to the Police Station. He looked at the telephone number and recognised it as Dan Dene's. He picked up the receiver and dialled, then waited a few seconds for the secretary at the other end to answer.

"Mr. Dene there, please?", said Bell.

"Who wants him?", said the nice sounding secretary.

"Mr. Bell".

"Just a moment Mr. Bell, I'll call him". There was a pause.

"Hello Harry, glad you got my message. The job looks like it will be on in the next day or so".

"Good", said Bell. "When is the stuff due?"

"We're due to take delivery tomorrow morning some time".

"Where is it coming from?"

"The Shipway Export and Import Company, Tilbury Docks. It's on dock eight".

"Good", said Bell. "Leave it to me".

"Good luck Harry", wished Dene.

Bell was too tired to want to do much, but he knew that he had to get things organised if he was going to get this load in the morning. He wanted this one badly and intended to see it through. He sought out Bill Peterson and told him he suspected that the lorry would be hijacked early in the morning, on its way from Tilbury to the Quality Sound Services warehouse in town.

Detective Chief Inspector Frost was more than interested in Bell's theory.

"Sounds good", he said. "Do you think we can nab them this time then?"

"I can Sir", said Bell, "with a little help".

"What's your plan then?"

"I hope to pick up the lorry as it leaves Tilbury, and follow it at a discreet distance. If the switch takes place alright, I'll follow on and see where it goes. That should lead us to the organiser and handlers. I'll need a couple of cars in addition to mine, so we can swap from time to time and not show out; those boys are fly ones, and we don't want to spoil it by having the same car following all the way".

"Alright", said Frost. "Peterson and Smith can go with you. What vehicles do you suggest you take?"

"Something nondescript I should think", said Bell. "What about the old van and the estate car; and I'll take the Hillman. I reckon between us we can do okay".

"Right then", said Frost. "That's settled. I'll leave you to make the arrangements".

"Thank you Sir", replied Bell, stifling a yawn.

Bell picked up Peterson and Smith and they went to the canteen to discuss their plan over a cup of stewed tea. They decided to meet at the Station at six o'clock the following morning, and drive to Tilbury. They could pick up the lorry as it left the premises. Shouldn't be too difficult to find out which one was carrying the gear for Quality Sound.

"How do you think they'll switch, Harry?", Peterson asked.

"I would say they'll switch at some transport cafe. Usual thing, the lorry will pull in and the driver will go for breakfast. When he comes out, the lorry will be gone. He'll have given it long enough to get a fair distance before he raises the alarm, by which time the lorry will be out of the way".

"Just like that, Harry?"

"Just like that - at least, that's how they usually go, especially when the driver is in collusion with the thieves, which is quite often".

Bell slept from early evening until five thirty the following morning. The sleep did him good and he felt quite refreshed when the 'phone awakened him and the operator announced that it was time for his early call.

"Thanks", he said, leaping out of bed and making for the shower. He freshened up and shaved and then dressed casually in old slacks and a roll neck sweater. He didn't want to look too much like a copper.

At six o'clock, Bell, Peterson and Smith met at the Station motor pool.

"Right then, a fast run down to Tilbury", said Bell. "Shouldn't take too long. You both know the drill".

The journey to Tilbury was not too bad. Traffic was building up but didn't impede them more than a little. They arrived near the entrance to eight dock at ten minutes past seven. Bell lounged against the wall by the gate, his old Hillman car a short distance down the road. Peterson sat on a wall a hundred yards further on, a newspaper held loosely in front of him, whilst Smith tinkered under the bonnet of the estate car further up the road.

From his vantage point, Bell could clearly see the premises of the Shipway Export and Import Company warehouse, right on the dock. A small compound at the rear, still locked, contained six covered lorries marked 'Ocean Import Services'. Just one vehicle was being tended by its driver. A man wearing a dust coat and holding a clip board, spoke to the man. They nodded and seemed to be talking secretively about something. The man in the dust coat was smart-looking, fair haired and hard faced. Somehow, he didn't strike Bell as the working kind. "Still, it takes all sorts", he mused.

The man in the dust coat unlocked the gates and the driver climbed into the cab of the large box truck. "Give us a ring and let me know how it goes", the fair haired man called to the driver as he began to roll.

"See you Frank", replied the driver, and the lorry rumbled out through the compound gates and headed towards the main gates. Bell saw the fair haired man relock the compound.

"This is it", he said, over his portable radio. "I'll take the first lead. Good hunting".

He jumped into the Hillman and made a show of starting up. He followed on behind the lorry as it headed down the street towards the main road. Smith and Peterson hung well back and allowed other vehicles to come between them. This was a tricky business and good use had to be made of the natural flow of traffic to cover their own presence. From time to time, they would catch up and the lead vehicle would drop away out of sight. Radio was their main asset.

After several miles, it became clear to Bell that the lorry was making for the A1 Northbound. As it turned on to the great stretch of road at the Mill Hill roundabout, Bell decided that it was time for him to drop out of sight again. He had been following with about four vehicles in front of him most of the way so far, but there was no point in pushing his luck. Smith came up and positioned three cars back from the lorry, now trundling along at fifty miles an hour. Peterson kept Smith in sight whilst Bell fell right back behind a couple of tankers. He knew that each change of route would be relayed to him by radio, so there was no need to keep in sight all the time.

"It's turning off onto the M10 motorway at Park Street", Bell heard over his radio. Smith was behind the suspect and doing a good job.

"Fine", said Bell. "Looks like we're going all the way. I should think the breakfast stop will come pretty soon. Keep your eyes about you".

It was Peterson's turn to take the lead now, and he pushed on ahead of Smith who dropped back half a mile or so. The lorry continued and then joined the M1 motorway. There was no need to worry too much, there was only one way the lorry could go so long as he kept to the motorway.

A short distance further on, Peterson informed his colleagues that the lorry was signalling a left turn.

"A5 coming up", he said. "Looks like it's turning off. Better close up a bit".

Sure enough the lorry turned off on the A5 and continued North for a few miles. Bell had again taken the lead and reported that the lorry was slowing down and signalling to go into a large transport cafe on the left.

"This could be it", he said. "Okay Smithie, you stop back there where you are. Bill, carry on up the road half a mile and get your bonnet up, okay?"

The two men acknowledged and Bell followed the lorry into the car park. He parked his car between two bulk grain carriers and got out. He noted that the suspect vehicle was parking at the very far end near the exit and in a position which concealed it from the cafe itself, by the presence of a big T.I.R. continental truck, big enough to hid a whole convoy.

Bell looked around and noted no more than three private cars in the park. One, a family tourer with suitcases on the roof rack. No bother there. A builder's van with planks of wood and ladders loaded all over the roof and on the sides. Bell took the number and description of a silver grey Cortina G.T. which was discreetly parked at the back of the cafe building. A brown trilby hat occupied the rear window shelf. He passed the number to his colleagues just for information, and waited. He lifted his boot lid and rummaged about in the back. He was able to look through the opening between the lid and the bodywork, and right through the window of his car. He could see the Cortina in one direction and the 'Ocean Import Services' truck in the other. No one would 'sus him out'.

The lorry driver got out of his cab and made a great show of locking the doors. He walked around his vehicle, then, satisfied, made towards the cafe, tucking his gloves into his hip pocket as he walked. He looked pleased yet a little nervous. He disappeared inside the cafe.

Three seconds later, two men came out. One, a smart looking fellow wearing flared grey trousers and a blazer over a roll-necked sweater. The other, walking slightly behind him as if they were not together, wore a reefer jacket and jeans with big brown boots. The smart looking man made straight for the Cortina and got in. He reversed and drove slowly out of the car park towards the North. Bell reported the movement and his colleagues waited for the next move.

The man in the reefer jacket was immediately recognisable to Bell, as Don Broadman. He was known, and Bell had picked up a recent photograph of the man from the Collator's office when he first got the tip from the barmaid. There was no doubt, Broadman was in on this job, just fine. Bell thought how like his brother Broadman was, except that Colin was slimmer and smarter.

Broadman looked about just once, then, removing a bunch of keys from his pocket, inserted one and opened the door of the cab. He climbed into the cab of the suspect lorry and the engine fired. The lorry rolled backwards into the main car park and then inched its way forward. A pause for traffic to pass, then out into the main road and Northwards on the A5.

"We're on the move", said Bell over his radio, the excitement showing in his voice. He climbed back into the Hillman and slowly drove out of the car park. He made no attempt to catch up with the lorry. He knew that Peterson would pick up the follow when the lorry went past him. Smith would already be on the move and Bell himself would tail along at a suitable distance. Things were going just fine. He began to feel a cloud lifting as he saw success coming his way at last.

The lorry continued up the road for a short distance, then suddenly, taken by surprise, Peterson reported that it was turning off again into a narrow, steep road leading up to his right.

"Go straight on by", Bell instructed; "Smithie, you follow, but for Christ's sake, keep your distance. We don't want to blow it now".

"Right", acknowledged Smith, and Bell saw the estate car turn to its right and go slowly up the hill, winding its way through trees and bushes. Bell wound his window down and then positioned himself to turn right also. He could hear the lorry grinding its way up the long incline. He radioed Peterson to turn round and follow up behind. He wanted enough support if needed. He parked at the bottom of the hill, in a field entrance, and waited for Peterson to come up. Peterson turned into the gateway and got out. Bell was locking his own car.

"Alright Bill", he said. "We're doing fine. I'm coming in with you from now on. Don't want too many cars giving the game away. Let's get up there and see what Smithie is doing".

"They didn't stay long on the main road did they?", Peterson remarked.

"No", said Bell; "and I doubt if they will be on the road at all, more than a few minutes. There must be a bloody good 'run in' here somewhere, and within minutes the thing will be concealed and unloaded. I doubt if the lorry will ever be seen again".

"How's that then?"

"Well, I've known lorry thieves to have a load away, drive to a lonely farm or similar place, conceal the lorry and load in a barn, and then unload. Within hours a team was cutting it up with torches and it went out as a bit of old scrap over a short period of time. They made a profit on that at the local scrap yard. They're a crafty breed Bill".

They came to a sharp right hand bend, and ahead of then, saw Smith's van concealed behind a large bush just off the road. Bill Peterson pulled over and they got out.

"Where the hell is he?", whispered Peterson.

"I don't know, but I hope he isn't going to play the bloody Sherlock Holmes bit all on his own. He'll blow the bloody lot".

They had no need to fear. Smith was just a few yards away in a small copse. He beckoned to them and they joined him, well under cover. Smith pointed towards a large barn at the rear of an old dilapidated farm house. The out buildings were falling down and there were several old farm implements littering the yard. The place hadn't been worked for years. A rumbling noise from inside the barn, indicated the presence of the lorry. Then the engine cut and there was silence. A clang told them that someone had bolted the large corrugated iron doors from inside.

The three Detectives looked at each other and grinned. They were quite elated by their successful operation, but the game was not played out yet. they still had to round up the team, and Bell particularly wanted to get to the top man - with sufficient evidence to convict him. He knew that the chance would come - if he played it cool and easy.

The next step would be critical, Bell knew; and he had to plan the best possible way to contain both the load and those responsible. He decided to leave Smith where he was, watching the premises, whilst he and Peterson made the arrangements for more men to join them in the next move. Smith didn't much like the idea of being left on his own. He had no means of communication, since the portables were only for car to car use, and covered a very limited range. However, he would have to put up with it until his colleagues could get more men to join them.

A movement from within made them stiffen and hold their breath. The figure of Don Broadman came out of the wicket door, and the smart man in the blazer followed. They locked up and walked around the back of the building.

"Quick Bill", said Bell. "Back to the car. They'll be coming out any minute. Where's the bloody entrance to this farm anyway?", he addressed Smith.

"Just up the road, there", Smith pointed.

"Right then, there's only one way out, this is a 'No Through Road', I saw the sign at the bottom of the hill. Come on Bill, let's get down to the bottom of the hill and see what happens".

They dashed back to the van and started up. Peterson drove directly to the bottom of the hill and crossed the main road to await their suspects, on the lay-by just beyond the junction. Seconds later, the silver grey Cortina appeared from the hill road and turned right onto the A5 again. Bell urged Peterson to get after them but, once again, at a discreet distance. They had a bit of a job keeping up with the fast car and the driver knew how to handle it. He slipped through a bundle of cars inching their way in and out of a junction on the left, and put another four cars between them and the Police vehicle. Nevertheless, Peterson managed to keep them in sight.

The two cars sped into the next town, a few miles up the road, and the Cortina turned into a car park beside a large public house. 'The Dick Turpin', sign swung from a bracket shaped like a gallows, and the picture depicting a highwayman on horseback, was lavishly coloured.

Peterson drove past and stopped in a slip road a hundred yards further on. Bell watched as the two men climbed out of the Cortina and entered the saloon bar of the public house.

"Come on Bill", said Bell. "Let's get over there and see if they're meeting anyone. I want to see everything".

They hurried back to the pub and went in, separately. Bell went into the public bar and Peterson went directly into the lounge bar. Each leaned on the respective counters and ordered beers. Peterson stood within five feet of the two men who had joined a third, a rather stocky man with dark hair, greying at the sides and about the temples. He was about forty, very expensively dressed and never smiled.

Peterson watched them in the mirror behind the bar as he sipped his beer.

Bell found that by leaning on the bar in the 'Public' he could just see the three men seated behind Peterson, via a serving hatch which joined the two rooms. He strained to see who the third man was, and suddenly froze as the cold eyes of Chandler swept the room. He didn't see Bell, and did not know Peterson. The three men got their heads together and for the first time, Chandler smiled. He patted both men on the shoulders as if praising them, and gave Broadman a fiver telling him to order a round of doubles.

Broadman sidled up to the bar and stood beside Peterson who buried his face in his pint glass. He ordered three double whiskies and seemed to be smiling all the while. "Have one yourself", he said benevolently to the barmaid.

Bell had seen enough to associate the hijackers with Chandler. He slipped out of the door and made for the public telephone kiosk outside. He dialled the office number and spoke to Frost.

"How did it go, Bell?", Frost asked in his usual manner.

"We got 'em Sir. At least, we followed them to a farm not far from home. They then left and are now sitting in the 'Dick Turpin' bar in Dunstley, only a few minutes away. They joined that fellow I told you about Sir - William Chandler".

"Good man!", snapped Frost suddenly, and Bell could imagine him sitting bolt upright.

"The thing is Sir", continued Bell. "We've left Smith up at the farm watching points whilst we followed these two villains to Dunstley. I think we ought to get someone up there to join him as soon as we can. Something is bound to move soon, and I fancy we can grab the lot of 'em when they go to unload and distribute".

"Right Harry. Now listen. Let's have the exact location, and I'll send a team of Crime Squad boys along, they can stake the place out and do what's necessary".

Bell described the layout of the farm and left the rest to Frost. He knew that Frost would get things moving from that end and Smith would have company within a very short space of time.

"What are you going to do now, Harry?", Frost asked.

"I'm not quite sure Sir", Bell replied. "But I want to nail Chandler somehow. He'll be bloody crafty and probably won't go near the place at all. I don't know if it will be any good following him".

"Well, you don't know where he operates from or even where he lives do you, Bell?", said Frost. "So I think it would be as well, now that you have located him, if you were to follow him and see where he goes. At least it will give you another lead on him".

"Thank you Sir. I think you're right - I'll do that then with Peterson".

"Of course, I'm right Bell - don't need you to tell me. Yes, alright, take Peterson with you, and mind how you go now".

"Right Sir", said Bell. "Oh, one other thing Sir. I've had to leave the Hillman at the side of the road at the bottom of the approach hill. Can someone pick it up and take it in please?"

"I'll see to it", said Frost. Bell hung up.

As he came out of the kiosk, he saw Broadman and his companion coming out of the saloon bar and head across the car park towards the Cortina. They were both smiling and looked very pleased. He watched them climb into the car and drive off, then crossed the road and joined Peterson who had also come out.

"Where's the big fellow?", Bell asked.

"Still in there on his own", said Peterson. "Do you know him, Harry?"

"I know him alright", replied Bell, cynically. "That's the bastard that had Susan beaten up".

"You mean.....?"

"Yes, Chandler. Remember I told you, he threatened to have her fixed if I didn't play along with him. Well, I'm going to bloody fix him good and proper, Bill. I'll have him eventually".

They returned to their car and watched the pub. Half an hour passed by and still no sign of Chandler. They began to get impatient.

"I'm getting a bit hungry", said Peterson, arching his back. "What's the time?"

Bell looked at his watch. "Christ!", he exclaimed. "It's only half past eleven".

The door swung open and Chandler came out of the pub. He walked confidently towards a large, green Daimler which was parked along the front wall. He unlocked the door and climbed in. The engine started and the car purred away from the car park, silently. He turned onto the main road again and headed North.

"Cop his number, Harry", said Peterson, turning the starter. The Daimler glided past them and Chandler didn't turn his head, just kept looking straight ahead. Peterson moved the car out into the stream of traffic behind a Ford Classic. A motor cyclist got in front of them and a pedal cyclist almost fell off as the old van cut in.

"Bloody maniac!", called the cyclist, shaking his fist at the undercover Police vehicle. At the same instant, he rode straight into the back of a stationary Mini and fell in a heap. Bell couldn't help laughing. It had been the fool's own fault for not looking where he was going.

"Where's the bloody Daimler?", Bell suddenly said, having lost sight of it temporarily.

"Alright", replied Peterson. "It's just ahead, in front of that bus, don't worry".

"Well for pete's sake, don't lose him", Bell snorted.

They drove on for a mile or so, then turned right at the cross roads and headed back towards their own patch. They passed the hospital and went under the motorway bridge, then turned left and through a dozen side streets until reaching a high class residential part of town. Peterson stopped and watched the Daimler turn into the drive of a big house two hundred yards along the road. Chandler got out and let himself into the large impressive looking house.

"So that's where he lives", breathed Bell. "Okay, Bill", he said, "back to the office".

Chapter 24

Smith was relieved at the sight of a dozen men who arrived silently and without announcement. They were fully briefed and ready to settle down for as long as necessary. They sorted themselves out in pairs at various points about the farm - in barns and at any vantage point available. They expected a long wait. Smith was joined by a Detective Sergeant of the Regional Crime Squad.

"Good load is it mate?", the Sergeant asked, settling down under the bush.

"About twelve thousand quid's worth", replied Smith. "Radio gear and the like".

"Who's the team then?"

"Don't rightly know. D.C. Bell is in charge of this one. Local team though".

"Bell's the bloke that shot that villain the other day ain't he?"

"Yes", said Smith.

"Bit of a mad bastard is he then?"

"No", said Smith. "He's a bloody good copper. At least he gets on and does the job and he isn't frightened to get stuck in".

"Huh", retorted the Sergeant. "Ain't been promoted though, has he?"

"That isn't his fault", said Smith, a feeling of disliking creeping over him. The Sergeant was obviously one of those 'know it all' types.

"Just my luck to get lumbered with someone like him", he thought.

The afternoon passed without event, and Smith became restless. He was hungry and tired and cramped. He was beginning to get fed up with the job and wished that something would happen, sharpish.

It was midnight before a relief team arrived, one at a time, and the tired observers left for their beds. Nothing had happened at all. It was no surprise. The team probably wouldn't return to the old farm until the heat was off and then they would move in and distribute the stuff without fear of detection.

Reg Tomlinson had been taken into the local Police Station where he had faced senior Detectives for several hours after reporting his load missing. He was, of course, immediately suspected of collusion.

He had stood firm for hours, sticking to the story that he had gone into the transport cafe for breakfast, coming out half an hour later to find his lorry gone. He had raised the alarm straight away. The Detective Superintendent of the Division had taken charge of the case himself, questioning Tomlinson who, admitting his part in the theft of the load, confessed to conspiring with a man he had met in a pub some time previous. He had been locked up and left to think about it in the hope that he would come up with more names and addressed. He held firm and involved no one else.

Chapter 25

Bell was back on duty again the following morning and went directly to the farm where he was joined by Peterson and a crowd of Crime Squad men. They relived the night watch and secreted themselves in hiding places previously occupied by their colleagues. Bell settled down with a morning paper and a flask of hot coffee. He said very little to Peterson who had put his feet up and laid back. He could just see the barn through the broken window of the old outhouse. The day had shown promise of being sunny, and life was beginning to stir. It was six thirty.

"Reckon we'll have 'em today then Harry?", Peterson asked. "I hope they aren't going to keep us hanging about too long".

"Could be today Bill", replied Bell, still deeply engrossed in his morning news.

"Well, there are enough of us to eat them if they come", commented Peterson.

Silence embraced the watchers once more, and to the casual observer, the farm premises were just empty and old and derelict. No one would have guessed that a dozen Detectives were concealed, awaiting their big moment.

I was nine o'clock when the first van arrived. A large thirty hundredweight plain, green van, drove into the yard and stopped outside the big barn. The driver, a tall scruffy youth, wearing a black leather jacket, climbed out. He walked to the corner of the barn and looked about him, then, oblivious of the dozen pairs of eyes which were watching him, blissfully urinated against the wall. He ambled back to the van and lit a cigarette.

Ten minutes later, a second van arrived, this time a grey twenty five hundredweight, with two men aboard. They drove over to the green van and the occupants got out and walked around to the first driver. Bell already had the first driver tagged; it was Bernard

Smedley, one of the White Cow crowd. The three men exchanged conversation and one of them looked at his watch impatiently.

Within the next fifteen minutes, two more vans arrived and a total of six men were gathered outside the barn door. The last man to arrive was unmistakeably the fair haired man who had supervised the departure of the load from Shipway Export and Import on the dock at Tilbury. He was no longer wearing his dust coat. Instead, he wore a white, impeccably pressed boiler suit. He carried a clip board on which flapped a bundle of papers. He seemed to be in charge, and after a brief conversation, he unlocked the doors and they all went in. Bell was able to get a better look at the men as they all filed into the barn - Smedley, Broadman, the fair haired supervisor type, and three others he did not recognise.

The big doors swung open and the lorry became visible within. The men went in and closed the doors behind them. There was a sound of a roller door being lifted as the men started work on the lorry. Unloading would probably take some time. The watchers waited.

An hour later, the doors swung open again and the first van was backed up to the doors. Bell could see the fair haired supervisor ticking off notes on his clip board as the others loaded the van with boxes of varying shapes and sizes. The van, eventually loaded, was driven out into the yard and left. The supervisor handed the driver a ticket which he placed in his jacket pocket. They returned to the barn and assisted the others in the loading of the other three vans. The job took four hours and each van was driven out into the yard on completion.

The job appeared to be complete, and it looked as though the vans would be driven off at any time. Bell decided that this was as good a time as any, to move in on the villains and arrest the lot of them. He signalled to the Detective Sergeant in the building opposite and the message was passed by portable radio to all the men lying in wait. As the gang went back inside for a final word, the Detectives came out of hiding and surrounded the barn. Bell and the Detective Sergeant went in first, followed by half a dozen men. There was a brief struggle.

"We are Police Officers", called the Sergeant. "Stay just where you are, all of you. The premises are surrounded and there is no way of escaping. You are all under arrest for being concerned in the theft and handling of this load".

The fair haired man made a dash for the door but Bell shot his foot out, caught him on the ankle and sent him sprawling in the dirt, messing up his clean white overalls. Bell pounced and handcuffed him without further delay. He was the man Bell wanted. He could obviously tell them more than any of the others, about the set-up. The struggle within the barn did not last long and there was very little effort put into the resistance. It was clear to the gang, that they could not get away. They gave up quietly.

A convoy of vans moved along the road and headed for the Police yard. The Detective Superintendent who had been questioning Tomlinson the previous day, was pleased that the waiting game was virtually over. He now had the ammunition to fire at the driver of the lorry. Bell, however, decided to push on with the fair haired man.

"What is your full name and address?", he asked the man now settled in an interview room at the Station.

"Find out", snapped the man.

"I'll bloody find out soon enough", retorted Bell, "but you're going to tell me. I'm not fooling around, playing bloody games all day. Now, who are you?"

"You want to know - you do the investigating, copper", hissed the man.

Bell didn't intend to play about all day. He had just about had enough of this job and he had waited long enough as it was. He adopted the move which most coppers steer clear of. He lost his temper and hit the man square on the jaw. The blow was so hard, that Bell's hand immediately bled where the knuckle had split. The man tipped backwards in his chair and fell onto the floor, hitting his head on a filing cabinet as he went. He grunted as the wind was knocked out of his lungs. Bell moved deliberately over to him and growled. "Come on, get up you bastard. I'm not finished with you, not by a long bloody way".

He grabbed the man and lifted him bodily, slamming him back into the chair. Bell grabbed the man by the hair and jerked his head backwards.

"You want to be the hard man do you?", Bell growled. "Okay then, we'll play the hard men shall we?". He lifted his bleeding hand and made as if to strike the frightened man again.

"No, no", the man said suddenly, cringing away from the threatened blow. "I'll tell you".

"Right then", said Bell. "Let's get down to it - and no more bloody mucking me about". He took pencil and paper and sat down.

"Name", he ordered.

"Weymes", whined the man. "Frank Weymes".

"Age?"

"Twenty eight".

"Where do you live?"

"I stay up at Grove Mansions with Mavis Jones".

Bell looked up sharply. "You live with Mavis Jones?", he said.

"Yes, why?"

"Christ man", said Bell. "You're in on that racket as well eh? She is a brothel keeper - so I guess that makes you guilty of living on immoral earnings too".

"Now listen here", began Weymes.

"No, you listen to me", interrupted Bell. "You're in no position to tell me what to do. Do you have any other address at all?"

"No".

"Good, that makes my job a little easier", said Bell.

Bell studied the clip board which he had taken from Weymes back at the warehouse. He flicked through the invoices and noted the names and addresses of the various receivers.

"All very business like, but all very stupid too", he thought.

Weymes was trapped. There was no way out of his predicament now. His only hope was to tell the Police what they wanted to know and hope for a light sentence. After all, if he played along with them, they might just put in a good word for him. He was no hero and saw no reason why he should be loyal to Chandler if it meant going down for a long stretch. Chandler certainly wouldn't lose any sleep over it and would not make any move to help him out.

He told Bell how the operation was to work and how he was to collect payment within a few days. The money should be forwarded to a box number which would not be made known to him until a later date. He did not know, he said, who the top man was. The others in the team were to be paid out of the money received by Weymes. They had set fees and the rest would then be forwarded to the top. Weymes would be paid in due course. He had no worries on that score.

Bell passed the information on to the Detective Superintendent who arranged for the expectant receivers to be arrested and charged with conspiracy. The operation was snow balling nicely.

Later that day, Bell and Peterson went to Grove Mansions on the fringes of the town. The building was tall and recently built. The exterior of white portland stone, was impressive and flower gardens were well tended by a full time gardener.

Bell pressed the bell add after a short wait, Mavis Jones opened the door. Bell flashed his warrant card.

"Police", he said flatly. "May we come in. We have something to discuss with you".

"I suppose you had better come in then", Mavis answered tartly, "don't want you discussing business out there on the doorstep". She stood aside and let them into the apartment which was expensively furnished. They stepped into the main living room, a spacious lounge with good quality furnishings. The carpet alone must have cost a fortune.

"Well, what is it you want?", she said, wrapping her gown around her otherwise unclad body.

"We've got a warrant to search the premises", said Peterson. He took the sheet of paper from his pocket and handed it to her. She read it without comment then handed it back to him. She said nothing.

"Where is Weymes's room?", asked Bell.

"We share", said Mavis, "any objections?"

"No, but we're going to search it, thoroughly, so I suppose you had better hang about whilst we do it".

"What's it all about then?", she asked. "What are you looking for?"

"Don't you know?", said Bell.

"Why should I?", said Mavis. "What is Frank supposed to have done? Is he under arrest or something?"

"He is under arrest and will be charged with numerous offenses ranging from conspiracy, theft and handling stolen property, to living on immoral earnings perhaps. Whatever, you are in no position at all to act indignant about it. Now, let's see his room", demanded Bell.

Mavis led them into the big bedroom. The wardrobes and cupboards had been built-in professionally, and provided a mellow background to the bright carpet and wallpaper. Bell started with the wardrobe at the far end, and Peterson made a start on the bedside cabinet. Dressing gowns and shirts fell to their scrutiny, every pocket in every garment, inside shoes and hat boxes, even the folds of Weymes's ties, were subjected to examination.

Bell was thorough. He knocked the walls and lifted loose fittings. He tipped out the drawers and pulled them right out of the frames and looked on the backs and bottoms and inside the fixtures themselves, for any sign of anything at all that might incriminate Weymes further.

"Aha!", exclaimed Peterson, opening a diary which he had taken from the bedside cabinet. He handed it to Bell.

Listed in the diary was a comprehensive selection of names, and alongside each name, a letter, and alongside that again, a sum of money. This list appeared in the 'Notes' section at the front of the diary. Bell thumbed through the diary and noticed that on the last day of each month, the initials W.C. appeared, together with a sum of money paid out.

A closer study of the diary, revealed Roger Bender's name together with the initials 'H', 'C' and 'P'. Bell studied the diary further then decided that they would take it with them and put it to Weymes direct.

He looked around the room. No more drawers or cupboards. His eyes fell upon the beautifully made bed. He grabbed the corner of the mattress and pulled it off, letting it drop onto the floor.

"Hey, watch it!", cried Mavis, grabbing at the bedclothes.

"We'll put it back", said Bell; "don't bother yourself".

"Just don't chuck the stuff about on the bloody floor", said Mavis. "We do have to sleep in it you know".

"Sure", said Bell, sarcastically.

He pulled the lining off the divan bed and revealed a stitched square, about two feet by two feet. A tape tag, hanging loose, was stitched to one side.

"What's this then?", Bell asked, glancing at Mavis.

Her face was serious and she looked just a little scared.

"Nothing", she said, softly.

Bell pulled the tag and the square opened and lifted out, revealing a deep compartment constructed in the bed itself. The compartment contained a couple of dozen cardboard boxes, each marked 'British Pharmacies Ltd.' He lifted out one box and opened it up. It contained packets of a white powdery substance. He looked up and saw fear in the eyes of the woman who was now, nervously twisting her dressing gown between her fingers.

"What is it?", Bell said.

"I don't know. Honest. Frank put it there".

"My bet is it's heroin", said Bell, tossing it to Peterson. "We'll take it".

He lifted out the other boxes, one by one. Half of them contained the same white substance. Others contained tablets of all colours and sizes, and a large plastic bag at the bottom, contained what was unmistakeably a block of cannabis.

Bell looked thoughtfully at the goods for some moments, then raised his eyebrows as if a thought had suddenly occurred to him.

"Got it", he said at last. "Those initials in the diary. 'H' for heroin. 'P' for pills and 'C' for cannabis. That bloody diary is a record of deals he has done in illegal drugs peddling".

"What about the 'W.C.' every month then?", asked Peterson.

"Don't know yet, unless......Christ!.....Bill, I wonder if it is.....could it be....yes, it all fits in. Remember the big fellow at the 'Dick Turpin' pub. Weymes is mixed up with that lot and Chandler seems to be the big boss. So it looks like Chandler is mixed up in drugs as well now. I like it Bill", said Bell. "I like it a lot". He rubbed his hands together eagerly.

They took Mavis with them for being in unlawful possession of drugs. After all, they were in her house, even though she denied knowing what they were - another likely story.

Bell and Peterson went into the cell and aroused Weymes from his sleep. Bell tossed the diary down and said nothing. Weymes picked it up and then looked up at the two Detectives, now standing straight faced, hands in pockets.

"Well", said Bell. "I want to know all about it".

"It's a diary", said Weymes, innocently.

"Oh!", replied Bell. "Well it isn't an ordinary diary is it?"

"What do you mean?", said Weymes, shaking a little now, his face a shade whiter than before.

"I know what it's all about", said Bell. "And he knows what it's all about. And now I want to hear you tell us what it's all about; and then I want a statement in writing, setting down all the implications and connections that this diary indicates - okay?"

"I don't know what you mean".

"Don't bloody fool around with us again, Weymes".

It was Peterson this time. "You're a right bloody villain, but worse still, you're a drugs pusher and that's the worst kind of villain there is. You're going to tell us all about your bloody rackets and who supplies you and how you get rid of the stuff. I want to hear every word. I want to know what makes a man like you tick, and how it is that you can encourage kids to take this muck. I want to see you cringe for your part in supplying this stuff to the pusher who supplied little Penny Whiteman with the dose that eventually killed her. Now bloody talk, or I might just forget that I'm a copper......".

Weymes shrunk back into the corner. He was sitting on the wooden bed, and felt certain that the two Detectives were going to tear him apart.

"Alright", he said at last, whimpering like a whipped dog. "I'll tell you it all. Can I have a cigarette please?"

Bell gave him a cigarette and lit it for him. He waited.

"Where shall I start?", Weymes asked.

"The beginning", said Bell.

"Well......", began Weymes.

"Wait a minute", Bell interrupted. "I suppose I'd better caution you. Do you know what that's all about?"

"Yes, I know", said Weymes.

"Good, you're cautioned", said Bell, "not that I want to see you take advantage of that little bit of rubbish - but I can say quite truthfully in Court, that you were cautioned, like the wise men say you should be. Okay, carry on".

"I've been working for this guy Chandler for a couple of years now. He's got interests everywhere. Chandler isn't his real name; that's just what he calls himself when it suits him. Well, he has these interests and a way of putting over any business deal. He deals with stolen loads and large scale thefts. He's crafty though. He rarely gets involved with the actual nicking or the negotiations".

"Who does that then?", asked Peterson.

"Well, I make a lot of the arrangements for the movement and handling of the stuff. He pays me well for my time and trouble. I just keep him informed".

"How?"

"He sends me a letter each week with a different P.O. box number where I can send messages to him. If I want him really urgent, I have a telephone number where someone can get to him, but only if it's very urgent".

"Would that number be 73529?", asked Bell, remembering the number that Chandler had given him at the outset.

"Yes, that's right - how did you know?"

"Never mind - go on".

"Well, I keep my ear to the ground and Chandler occasionally gives me a specific job to do. He arranged for me to get a supervisor's job at Shipway Export and Import. He knows someone in the firm and told them that he wanted an old friend fixed up with a good job. They obliged - didn't know the real reason. I was there so that I could make the arrangements behind the scenes for the hijacking of that load. It's worth a few grand".

"What about the drugs?", asked Bell. "All about it".

"Look mister. Am I going to go down for a long stretch over this lot?", asked Weymes. "I mean, I don't mind helping you now that you've got all the evidence, but I don't fancy facing Chandler or his henchmen after this".

"You'll be going away for a while", said Bell. "Now, the drugs".

"Chandler started me on that racket. He put me in charge of distribution of the stuff. I meet the pushers whenever they want. I supply them with the goods and they pay me on the spot. Chandler delivers the stuff to me once a month and I pay him an agreed price for the lot. I sell it at my own price and what I make on the deal is my own".

"How do the pushers contact you?"

"Easy. I just visit the discos and cafes and bars, two or three times a week and let them approach me. Then, I arrange to deliver".

"Are you a junkie Weymes?"

"Me? No, never. I wouldn't touch the stuff".

"But you encourage kids to take it". It was a statement.

"Well, I don't force them".

"No, you don't force them. But having started them off, they force themselves because they can't help themselves. And you keep feeding that need".

"Look Mr. Bell, I've told you what you wanted to know. Don't be my judge as well. Okay, so I've made a bomb on the rackets. But, I'm not giving you a hard time, am I?"

"You'd better not bloody try either", said Peterson.

"What was Colin Broadman's part in the organisation? You know, the guy who beat up my wife", said Bell, harshly.

"I'm sorry about that Mr. Bell. I don't like violence myself. Broadman is a sadist. He loves inflicting pain, especially on women. He would have given your wife a really bad time if you hadn't got there when you did. I'm glad he's out of the way".

"What was his job?"

"Chandler employed him to collect his debts. He had a lot of people paying blackmail - small time shopkeepers who he had hooked in his game of money lending which led on to handling stolen gear. Chandler was taking half of their profits in order to keep quiet about the crooked deal which he had pushed them into. Broadman collected. He also did any thumping that had to be done. Chandler was a very strong disciplinarian and wouldn't stand for any nonsense within the organisation".

"Who was the one that got away when I caught Broadman that night?"

"I don't know. I had very little to do with that side of the job".

"Alright Weymes", said Bell, finally. Satisfied that the story was now wide open, he just wanted the final points cleared up.

"I want that lot in writing now, under caution. Detective Peterson here will take it down, okay?"

"Yes, I'll make a statement".

"Good. See you later then". Bell walked out feeling good inside. At last, things seemed to be getting together and satisfaction was going to be his, soon.

Chapter 26

Harry Bell stood before the Coroner's jury whilst the Coroner himself cross examined him about the incident at Burnham Beeches. The facts had been related and the Forensic Scientist had given evidence proving that the bullet that had killed Lance Rodway was from the gun which Bell had handed to the Inspector after the shooting. Bell gave his version of what had happened, as did the Superintendent and the other Officers present.

"Mr. Bell", said the solicitor representing the family of the deceased. It was Mr. Rodgers, the same advocate who had defended Bimbo Parks. "We have met in Court before, and I have no desire to cast any doubts as to your integrity. I merely wish to seek the truth of this tragic matter. Would you tell the jury just how much firearms training you have received in the Police Force, and exactly what your position is with regard to the issue of guns".

Bell thought about his answer for several seconds. Then he looked at the jury and took a breath.

"Like most Police Officers", he began, "I have received very little training in the handling of firearms. Hitherto, there has been little need for such training in this country. I have, however, received a five day training course on the use of firearms in tactical situations. I am not what you might call a 'Marksman', but I know which way to point a gun and how to use one. I receive refresher training and a compulsory requalification shoot at regular intervals".

"But are you an expert, Mr. Bell?", asked the man Rodgers.

"Is anyone an expert at killing, Sir?", Bell replied.

The Coroner lifted his eyes and looked over the top of his glasses. Bell reflected how funny it was, that judges, magistrates and coroners, all seemed to do that. He wondered if it was part of their training - a kind of representation of authority from high places.

"Mr. Bell", the Coroner was saying, "I don't think that remark was called for".

"I'm sorry Sir", said Bell.

"Now Mr. Bell", continued Rodgers. "When you aimed that gun at Mr. Rodway on that fateful occasion, what was in your mind?"

"I saw him pointing his gun at the Superintendent. He had already wounded a Constable. He had fired several wild shots at us in the woods. He came out holding his gun and clearly threatened to shoot Mr. Gray. I saw his finger actually tightening on the trigger. I intended to stop him from shooting Mr. Gray".

"Come now Officer", said Rodgers. "You actually saw his finger tighten on the trigger? I can't believe that".

"I saw it Sir".

"And you shot him, intending to kill him?"

"I shot him, intending to hit him. I aimed at his chest and shoulders".

"Did you not call upon him to put down his gun?"

"All the warnings had been given. All the talking was over. He was going to kill my Superintendent".

"Kill, Mr. Bell? Kill? How can you be sure of that".

"As sure as you appear to be, that it was my intention to kill Rodway".

"You are impertinent Mr. Bell".

"And you Sir, are being presumptuous - with respect", said Bell, glaring at the solicitor.

Once more the Coroner interjected. "Gentlemen, we are here to ascertain certain facts. It is not my wish to have the characters of yourselves bandied about in this Court. Officer, please answer the questions and reserve your remarks for a later date".

"Yes Sir", sighed Bell.

"You didn't like Rodway, did you Officer?", said Rodgers.

"I don't think that question is a fair one Sir", said Bell.

"In fact, you hated the sight of him didn't you? He assaulted you, and you made up your mind to get back at him one way or another. Isn't that so?"

"Sir, as a Police Officer, I have learned to divorce my personal feelings for a person, from the job in hand. The fact that I may have liked or disliked him, has no bearing on the fact that I shot him.

However, he did receive fair warning which he chose to ignore. In spite of those warnings, he came out shooting and intended to harm my colleagues. I did what any other Officer would have done. It was unfortunate that my shot killed him".

"I understand that there were six men carrying firearms on that occasion".

"Yes Sir".

"Yet they did not see fit to shoot".

"I cannot answer for them Sir. Every Officer has to make up his own mind at the time. I made up my mind before they did, I suppose".

"Because you were eager to do so?"

"No Sir".

The issues went on and further evidence was called and submissions were made. The jury went out and returned after an hour and a quarter. The foreman expressed the verdict of them all.

"Justifiable homicide", he said, when asked by the Coroner.

The Coroner called upon Bell to stand. He addressed him, and the press reporters took down his words, hanging on to every phrase, every syllable and every intonation.

"You have been cleared by this Court Mr. Bell, and I fully agree with that verdict. I am convinced that the jury has reached the right decision. This unfortunate tragedy was a direct result of the deceased's own foolishness. However, it is always disturbing when a person is shot dead at the hands of the Police, and I feel it necessary to comment upon the subject of higher training within the Police Service, if such tragedies are to be stopped or reduced. We live in a violent age and it is becoming more and more apparent that violence must be met with violence; but we must take care not to replace the death penalty, already abolished, with summary execution at the hands of our Police Forces".

Bell was serious and his eyes looked heavy and bloodshot. He felt an intense desire to sleep and it must have showed. The Coroner continued.....

"Mr. Bell, I do not wish to appear personal, but I cannot help noticing that you seem to me to be very much in need of sleep. How much sleep have you had in the past week or so?"

"merely a few hours Sir", said Bell. "I have been extremely hard pushed. I have been working on more than one investigation and, of necessity, my hours have been much longer than usual".

"I see", said the Coroner. "Well, I hope that it cannot be said that it was because of your lack of proper rest, that this particular incident resulted as it did. A tired man with a firearm is not the safest of men".

On this sour note the Court was closed and the reporters hurried off to contact their editors. Bell could imagine the local papers making a big issue of the whole affair. It would, no doubt, lead to a demonstration by the usual factions of extremist groups demanding a public enquiry into the arming of our Police Forces. The usual chanting of 'Down with the Fascist Pigs', and 'Police Murderers should be prosecuted', and variations of the theme. There would be poison pen letters and public criticisms and all the rotten reactions of those whose aims are to disregard the causes of certain Police actions, and to demand restitution for an act which was necessary in the enforcement of the law and the protection of society in general.

Bell stepped down from the witness box, walked slowly out of the Court, and felt the rain beginning to drop from the grey sky. A grey day for a grey mood. A reporter pestered him for his full name and rank and something of his previous service in the force.

"I'm not able to answer any of your questions", Bell said. "You heard it all in there".

"But just a bit of your history Mr. Bell; we'd like to give you a write up".

"Look", said Bell. "You want anything on me - go see my guv'nor. Don't ask me".

He walked away and climbed into the Police car which was waiting to take witnesses back to Bell's own station. They had come down that day to the little village near Burnham Beeches, for the purpose of giving evidence at the Coroner's Court. Now they waited until all the stragglers were ready to return.

"Where is everyone?", the uniformed driver said to Bell as he climbed into the waiting car.

"Gone for a bloody drink, I suppose", said Bell, sinking into the corner of the seat, closing his eyes as he did so.

"Christ, I suppose we'll be waiting around for another hour for them then", said the driver. He looked at Bell and tossed his head on seeing that he wasn't even going to have the pleasure of the company of someone to talk to. He left the motor and joined the other drivers across the yard. Bell was already sleeping.

Chapter 27

Two days later, when Bell went into the office, he was greeted, not with warm smiles, but by the cold glare of Chief Inspector Frost.

"Come straight into my office, Bell", Frost ordered. "And shut the door behind you".

"What the hell have I done wrong now", Bell thought, following his master in through the thin door. He closed the door and went to take a seat.

"I didn't tell you to sit down Bell", snapped Frost, who also remained standing. "You have let me down. I thought you were sensible and discreet. I have always considered you a credit to the department".

"What is all this about Sir?", snapped Bell, surprised at the attack.

"The Assistant Chief Constable will be seeing you in the Chief Superintendent's office shortly. He'll tell you".

"Well don't you know what it is, Sir?", asked Bell, now even more concerned. He thought at first, that it was something to do with the comments of the Coroner at the inquest on Rodway, but somehow, dismissed the idea. It was just too ridiculous.

"Look Sir", he went on, raising his voice, "If you've got something on me then I'm entitled to know. Don't just shout and rave at me unless you have something to say Sir. I've worked bloody hard for you, especially over the last six months. I've lost my wife for you and your department - I've been beaten up through being conscientious. So don't treat me like one of the villains we're paid to catch".

"That's enough of that Bell", said Frost. He seemed somewhat embarrassed.

"Well then Sir", Bell asked again. "What's going on?"

"I'd rather leave it to the Assistant Chief", said Frost. "Now just wait patiently".

Bell waited for half an hour and the atmosphere in the outer office was electrified. No one knew what was going on and they were all concerned for their colleague, Bell.

At ten o'clock, the summons came and Frost told Bell to accompany him to the Chief Superintendent's office. They went up the stairs and along the passageway, and Frost knocked on the door. The little traffic light about the door turned to green, and Frost entered.

"Detective Constable Bell, Sir", he announced, and Bell walked smartly into the spacious room. His feet were silenced by the plush green carpet, and he came face to face with the Assistant Chief Constable, a tall, smart, distinguished looking man who knew how to wear a uniform well. He was sitting behind the great desk and the Chief Superintendent had been pushed to the armchair beside the window.

Bell stood to attention and looked directly at the Assistant Chief Constable. It wasn't often in a man's career, that he came face to face with the hierarchy, and one always felt a little humble in such distinguished company.

"I don't suppose you have any idea why you are here Bell, have you?", the Officer started. It became immediately apparent to Bell, that the Officer did not like him; at least, he felt the contempt in the man's attitude. He was uncomfortable already.

"No Sir", said Bell.

"Well I'll tell you Bell. I have received, via the Chief Constable, and allegation of misconduct by you. I have also received a photograph together with the complaint, and I understand that there are quite a lot more of this kind. He slipped a large, colour print across the table to Bell.

"Look at that Bell. Do you agree that that is you in the picture?"

Bell took the picture and gasped. He just couldn't believe it. Sure enough, it was him, lying on a large bed, completely naked, with three beautiful women. The picture showed him in gross sexual compromise. He shuddered and recognised the lovely body of Ruby. He swallowed and his throat burned dry.

"Well!", said the Assistant Chief.

"Yes Sir, it is me. But I haven't the slightest idea how that picture came to be taken".

"Oh come now man. Do you expect me to believe that you know nothing of such an incident?"

"Sir, I swear, I did not cooperate with the taking of that picture. I can only assume.....". He stopped short.

"Well", said the Officer. "Go on".

"I have been set-up, Sir".

"Oh now Bell - what do you think you are giving me?"

"Alright Sir", Bell said. "I went to a party some time ago. Not because I needed to, or because I was associating with anyone there. I went in the course of an investigation to try to track down a drugs pusher".

"I see. So that visit will be in your desk diary then, won't it".

"No Sir".

"Why not? Surely you know enough about the keeping of diaries to know that any duty visit or operation should be fully entered?"

"Well, that's just it Sir. Although it was in the course of my investigations, officially, I was off duty that night".

"I see - go on Bell, you intrigue me". His tone was cold.

"The fact is Sir, I was doped or something and although I could recall being undressed and these three women getting on to the bed with me, I was helpless to do anything about it. I woke up the next morning in my own bed at my own house and naturally, assumed that I had dreamed it all".

The Assistant Chief Constable was now leaning back comfortably in his chair, his hands entwined together and his thumbs chasing each other around in circles. There was a sickening look on his face as he listened to Bell's unbelievable story.

"Some story Bell", he said when Bell had finished. "That's children's stuff. You look happy enough in the picture - in fact you are smiling!"

Bell wanted to say 'wouldn't you be smiling too Sir, in that position', but thought better of it, He could see it all now. What a fool he had been. And what hurt, was that Ruby was in on it too. He had grown fond of her in a professional sort of way. He regarded her as a warm and sensuous person to whom he could go when he needed to be lifted. He didn't believe that she could double-cross him like this.

"The complaint is anonymous Bell, but the writer claims to be an influential person about this town. He claims that you are having affairs and associating with persons that make you a grave risk to security. You are, he claims, mixed up in blackmail and pornography. What have you to say?"

"I have nothing to say at all Sir, except that I deny such allegations, most strongly".

"Very well then. On the face of it, we have an unsupported allegation from an anonymous informant. At the most, I can accuse you of indiscreet sexual activity. You are a married man aren't you, and I don't want that sort of thing going on in this force. I'll have no more of this sort of thing Bell, do you hear?"

"Yes Sir", Bell said. He knew that there was no point in arguing. Someone had fixed him up and he had a good idea where he could start. No use in trying to defend himself. The evidence was there in full colour.

"That's all - get out", said the Assistant Chief, and Bell turned smartly on heel and toe, and left the room. He felt hot and weak, and his palms sweated. His parting memory was the Assistant Chief saying to the Chief Superintendent something about "Where do we get men like that?"

As he returned to his own desk, Bell felt the weight of the last few weeks bending his back a little more. The muscles in his shoulders ached and the heaviness behind his eyes, dragged the lids together a little closer. The feeling of depression began to nag at his mind, and he knew that someone was turning the big screw on the torture rack which was beginning to stretch his tolerance. The pressure was on now, coming on harder each day - but he knew that he had to break the chain that kept Chandler and his team dangling in front of him, like the carrot of so many tales of temptation. Whatever else happened to him, Bell was going to see it through - he hoped.

Chapter 28

It was four o'clock the same afternoon when the Detective Chief Inspector's telephone rang.

"I wish to make a complaint, the caller said. It was a man. "I am being blackmailed by a Detective. Can't give you his name. I haven't got much time now but I've just received a telephone call from him, telling me to bring another two hundred and fifty pounds to him this evening. I've got to dash around to raise it somehow. Look, I can't go on like this much more, you've got to stop it".

Frost intercepted the man's flow of babble.

"Who are you Sir?", he asked.

"My name is Wilkins", said the voice. "Look, I've got to meet this Detective at eight o'clock in the car park at the 'Old Rose Bush' pub on the A6. You know the place?"

"Yes"

"Well, he says to be there at eight o'clock sharp. He'll be in his car. I can't tell you his name. He just calls himself Harry. I don't know what his other name is".

"How long has this been going on?", asked Frost.

"About nine months now Sir", said the man.

"You'll have to make a statement if we catch him", said Frost.

"Of course I will", said the voice. It sounded frightened.

"Alright Mr. Wilkins. Leave it with us. You make sure you meet him and we'll be there. Don't worry about it".

"Thank you Sir", said the voice, and the line went dead.

Half an hour later, the telephone on Bell's desk rang. Bell put down his pen and stretched, then lifted the receiver to his car.

"Bell", he said "C.I.D."

"Oh good. I'm glad I found you in, Mr. Bell", said the sweet sounding voice. "I need to see you, tonight. It is urgent".

"Who are you, then?", Bell said, interested in the voice which sounded full of promise.

"You don't know me yet, Mr. Bell. But there's no reason why we shouldn't become friends".

"Look, what's all this about?", said Bell. He was intrigued by the voice.

"It's about my sister", the girl said. "You know - Penny Whiteman. I'm Joyce".

"Ah.....I see", said Bell. "I didn't know she had a sister".

"Well, here I am", said the voice. "Now Mr. Bell - will you meet me at the 'Old Rose Bush' pub out on the A6, say eight o'clock tonight, if you can make it. I'll see you there. Perhaps if you wait in the car park, I'll be able to recognise you. What car do you drive?"

"Old Austin", he said, and he gave her the number.

"Fine", the girl said, "then you'll meet me?"

"Sure - I'd love to".

"Thank you Mr. Bell. I'll see you then. Eight o'clock. Bye now".

"Just a minute............hello". The line burred - dead.

Bell put the receiver in the cradle and sat back thoughtfully.

"Why?", he thought, "would Penny's sister suddenly appear on the scene and want to see me. What could she possibly have to discuss with me. Still, I suppose there is a lot she could want to know about her sister - stands to reason - sure, she must want to know all about it".

He made up his diary and squared up his desk. He straightened a few papers and then went out of the office. He walked slowly to the car park and unlocked his old car. An early night was welcome and he took advantage of the temporary lull in pressure.

On the way home, he churned over in his mind, the ironic turn of events which seemed to have overtaken him. The criticism of the Coroner - the false allegations of the anonymous person and the photographs - the suspicion that Ruby had played a part in taking him for a sucker, and had conspired to compromise him - the breakdown of his marriage. Sue hadn't contacted him for quite a time now and he had done nothing more to reconcile their situation. Things had happened fast, and for the first time in his life, Bell had realised that he had been unable to control his affairs satisfactorily.

He changed down into second gear as he entered the large roundabout and for a moment he concentrated upon the traffic. A heavy T.I.R. truck thundered around the island and ploughed its way across the path of all the cars and cycles negotiating the hazard. The heavy monster did not yield one little bit to the other traffic.

"Bloody foreigners", Bell muttered. "Soon we'll be overrun by Frenchmen and Italians and Germans, and our traffic laws will all be changed to suit them. The Common Market will have wiped out our identities as Englishmen, and we'll all be driving on the wrong side of the road and trying to read signs that mean nothing to us. Next, I suppose, we'll all be ordered to learn to speak a Continental language and phase out English altogether".

He frowned and accelerated out of the roundabout, and continued along the main road. He lapsed back into his bleak thoughts once more.

"What the hell does a woman expect from a man?", he mused. "Sue knew that I was a copper when she married me. She knew I wouldn't be a nine to five man with every weekend off. She was happy enough to boast about being engaged to a Policeman, and loved the status whenever we went to a social event. But, she wanted the cake and the bloody cream. Bloody women!"

It was still raining as he turned into the small drive in front of his middle class semi-detached house on the outskirts of the town. It was a pleasant area, and the neighbours were friendly enough, although it had taken a very long time before they accepted him and Sue as one of them. Another draw back in a copper's life.

Bell opened the door and sifted through a heap of letters on the hall carpet. Electricity bill, garage bill, a birthday card to someone he had never even heard of. Nothing from Susan - not that he expected anything really, but he always looked and rather hoped. He didn't want a divorce. He still loved Susan and felt sure that after the separation, she would come to her senses and come home to him. They hadn't been married long enough to get bored with each other and they had done pretty well so far.

He dropped the mail on the kitchen table and poured himself a drink from the cocktail cabinet.

"I ought to give this up too", he thought. "Drinking too much these days".

He sipped the strong liquor and grimaced. He opened the fridge door and turned up his nose at the sight of bacon and eggs and sausages again.

"Wouldn't mind eating out", he thought; "but what fun is it eating alone?" He thought about Penny's sister and wondered if she would like to share a meal with him somewhere. "What did she say her name was? Joyce, that's it. Nice name - Joyce". He muttered to himself as he moved about the kitchen , pricking the sausages and heating up the fat. "How the hell can I vary the menu with the same stuff all the time?", he thought. "'suppose I could make the egg into an omelette - I wonder what it would be like with chopped sausage in it instead of ham?"

A piece of burnt toast with a broken fried egg, crisp bacon and burnt, burst sausages, adorned the large, unwarmed plate on a bare table. Bell looked at it and sighed. He sipped his whisky again and made a brave attempt to tackle the meal he had so terribly devastated.

"Bloody ulcers will be the next thing, I suppose", he moaned.

He switched on the television and tried to concentrate on the news. The newscaster was babbling on about the economy and some conference the Union bosses were attending in Blackpool. A feature on women's dress designs and a bit about some upper crust wedding.

"What a load of crap", he spat, switching off the set. He turned the radio and immediately winced as a popular group of noisemakers shouted and screamed their message to the younger generation. He switched off and dug his hands in his pockets. It was hopeless.

"How could a man relax in his own home, when it was no longer a home in the true sense of the word. What else then?"

Harry Bell was indeed a dejected man. He stripped off his shirt and threw it into the washing machine with the rest of the week's washing. Then he stripped off completely and chucked the lot into the spinning water and let it wash itself whilst he had a shower. From time to time, he went into the kitchen to supervise the machine and its contents. He shaved and made himself a little more presentable. He tried to sing but found himself unable to remember the words or the correct melody.

"Thank Christ I'm going out to see someone tonight", he said to himself at last. "I'll go bloody mad if I stay in this house too long. Might just as well be at work - at least I'd be doing something and meeting someone else to talk to".

He began to realise how it must have been for Susan, alone for hours on end in the house whilst he had been on duty. At least he had people to talk to, what had she got once she arrived home from her daily work? He realised why it was that she had become so bad tempered each time he had told her that he had to work late. What a blind fool he had been, not to have known how she felt.

At last it was time to go out. He got into the old car, feeling much better having cleaned up and changed his clothes. He drove out of town at a leisurely pace and switched on the radio. A decent bit of music for a change, drifted out of the speaker, and he hummed to the old fashioned tune on three dozen violins. It relaxed him and he felt eager to make the new acquaintance of Joyce Whiteman. He wondered what she would look like. He guessed that she would probably be a respectable girl with a good, secure job somewhere far away from this town. An innocent girl, with little knowledge of the sort of life that Penny had led. He didn't want to be the one to tell her about the drugs and the depravity and degradation that had driven her sister to her untimely death. Or the terrible ordeal at the hands of those animals, that had been her last contact with human beings. How do you tell such things to an innocent, decent person?

Bell could see the pub sign with a large, pink rose, swinging in the breeze. The sign was illuminated from inside and the rain slanted down across the road ahead, making an oblique pattern in the headlights. He slowed down and signalled a right turn, then swung slowly onto the forecourt of the 'Old Rose Bush' public house.

The car park was deserted except for a mediocre Ford Zephyr which was parked at one end. He didn't recognise the car, but then, why should he? He looked at his watch as he switched off his engine. Five minutes to eight - as usual, five minutes early for an appointment. That had always been his rule.

He listened to the radio and settled back with a cigarette to await the arrival of Joyce Whiteman. The wait seemed interminable, but he had grown accustomed to waiting patiently; it was part of his job. The rain continued to fall and the night was dark and miserable. His windows steamed up and he wiped a hand across the windscreen in order to see ahead. All was darkness.

The passenger door suddenly opened and a stocky figure slipped into the seat beside Bell. The man did not directly look at Bell who sat there, surprised and annoyed at the intrusion. The man settled and turned to face Bell. Recognition turned Bell's expression into an unpleasant scowl.

"What the hell do you want?", he said, switching on the interior light.

William Chandler smiled. "My dear Bell. I thought you would have been pleased to see me, especially since you instructed me to come here tonight". He smiled.

"What are you on about, Chandler?", Bell demanded. "I didn't come here to see you".

"But of course you did Mr. Bell", Chandler went on, reaching his hand into an inner pocket. "I do hope you won't make any more demands on me - I just can't afford to go on paying these large sums of money Mr. Bell. You must stop bleeding me like this. I think I would have preferred prosecution for that silly little offence nine months ago. Don't you think I've paid you enough for letting me off Mr. Bell?" Chandler's voice was pleading and Bell was confused and completely out of the picture.

"Here is your money Mr. Bell", Chandler said, handing the bundle to Bell who automatically wrapped his hand around the thick wad, not knowing what it was or what was happening. It was a reflex action really, the sort of action that anyone would take it someone handed a bundle to them.

Bell looked down at his hand, still holding the bundle of bank notes. At the same moment, his door was opened from outside and a torch shone directly onto his hands.

"I'll take that Bell", said a familiar voice. It was Frost. "I have heard everything that has gone on, and Detective Inspector

Summers here, can corroborate my evidence. You are not obliged to say anything unless you wish to do so Bell, but whatever you do say will be put into writing and may be given in evidence. I am detaining you for receiving a bribe; blackmail Bell - I'm sorry, but I've no choice".

Bell was dumbfounded. He looked from Frost to Chandler who was putting on a good act of being frightened. He couldn't speak, but gradually, the penny dropped and realisation made itself clear. He had, once again, been well and truly set up.

"Sir........I think you have it all wrong", he started. "I've been framed....set up....fixed....can't you see Sir. This is Chandler, the man I told you about".

"That will do Bell", said Frost. "You can leave your car here for now. I'll have uniform branch bring it into the Station. You are coming with me".

Bell looked at Chandler and saw the evil grin on his face.

"I'll bloody fix you Chandler", he hissed. "I've got the lot on you and I'm going to see you in hell, you bastard". Chandler merely grinned more.

"When would you like my statement Chief Inspector?", Chandler asked.

"I think in the circumstances, you had better come to the Station tonight Sir", said Frost.

"Very well", said Chandler, pretending to be nervous. "I'll follow you down".

"Right then", said Frost, and he started the Ford Zephyr which had been parked in the corner. He had only recently acquired the car and Bell had no reason to suspect that its presence meant anything sinister.

"Look Sir", Bell said as they drove. "I don't know what's going on, but I've been properly set up. I wasn't receiving a bribe, or blackmailing that man. He pushed the bundle into my hands - I didn't know what it was".

"You accepted it Bell".

"Christ! I didn't know what it was. He shoved it into my hand. How can you say I accepted it. I told you that man is William Chandler".

"That man is called Wilkins, and he has made a very serious complaint Bell".

"Maybe he has Sir, but it is a false complaint".

"Sorry Bell, the matter has to be thoroughly investigated".

Bell was silent for the rest of the journey. He was shocked and utterly miserable at the sequence of misfortune which had victimised him.

Detective Superintendent Gray interviewed Bell at the Station.

"An allegation has been made against you Bell; that nine months ago, you discovered a Mr. Wilkins committing an offence in a public convenience. This offence was not serious in itself, but one which might be detrimental to the man if disclosed publicly. The allegation goes on to say that you identified yourself to the man as a Police Officer, and you detained him and drove with him to a car park not far away. You then told him that unless he paid you two hundred pounds, you would take him to the Police Station and charge him with the offence of Gross Indecency in a public place. It is further alleged that he paid you two hundred pounds the following day and that since that date, you have demanded no less than six other payments from him, all of large sums of money totalling, to date, some eight hundred pounds, in return for your silence". He looked at Bell, rather sadly. "It's a great pity Bell".

Bell shrugged his shoulders. "What can I say Sir. I can't disprove such an allegation, unless you want to see my bank book. I run an old beat up car and don't spend lavishly. I am an honest copper Sir. I can give you reasons for such an allegation, but I cannot disprove them".

"What reasons Bell?"

"That man's name is really William Chandler. He collared me once and told me that he was the head of a large organisation with many interests. He suggested that they were criminal interests. He threatened to harm my wife unless I passed on to him, any information concerning Police activity connected with warehouse breaks and large scale thefts etc. He set me up with duff information once before and I didn't report to him. I later found two of his thugs beating up my wife, just like he threatened. I got my wife to the coast. She's still there now for all I know".

"Go on", urged Gray.

"Well, as you know, recently I've got mixed up in all sorts of jobs and I am certain that Chandler is behind them all. Penny Whiteman's death is even connected. He supplies the big bulk of all the drugs in this area, for illegal distribution, and it was from that source that Penny bought hers. He organised the big hijacking job I'm involved in too. I have enough evidence on him to pick him up and get stuck into him Sir. I have my report fully prepared. It is in the typist's office right now. Well, it is quite clear to me, that Chandler knows I've busted his racket wide open. He knows that I refused to play ball with him, so he has set me up. I even believe that that photo of me in bed with three women, was engineered by him too. I happen to know that the girls in that photo are being run by Mavis Jones, a brothel keeper. Her boy friend is Frank Weymes, Chandler's hatchet man. He's the one who has spilled the whole story. It's not too difficult to work out that Mavis put the girls in to that party. Marshall, the guy who threw the party, had big contacts and knew that he could get protection when I threatened to arrest them all on drugs charges. He had me doped and then organised the sex pictures. So they went back to Mavis and Weymes who passed them on to Chandler who recognised me and - well you can take it from there. He saved them for a rainy day Sir".

"That's an interesting theory Bell. Can you prove any of this?"

"Just about all of it Sir, providing Weymes will repeat it all in Court".

"Ah, but supposing he won't".

"Then I have to get the necessary evidence myself Sir. We could search Chandler's drum".

"And do you think you'll find anything there?"

"No. I don't suppose he's that stupid".

"Exactly. So let's get back to his allegations shall we?"

"Alright Sir".

"Right - now then, why did you go to the Old Rose Bush tonight Bell?"

"I had a phone call Sir, from a woman. She said her name was Joyce Whitemen, Penny's sister. Said she wanted to discuss Penny with me".

"Why there?"

"I don't know. She suggested it".

"Did she arrive?"

"No, of course not - she was obviously a decoy".

"Why did you want to discuss Penny. You knew that the case was cleared up?"

"Yes Sir, I know. But she sounded so genuine. Anyway, it was she who wanted to discuss Penny, not me".

"Aha yes - and you fell for it, eh?"

"Yes Sir".

"Why didn't you take a Police woman or even another Detective?"

"I was off duty Sir. Thought I could mix pleasure with useful socialising".

"You're a fool Bell".

"They're breaking me Sir. I don't like it and I feel so helpless right now. I wish I could do something more constructive - I can't. But I wish you would read my report Sir. It breaks open just about all of Chandler's rackets. We can pick him up any time, I know where he lives, I followed him the other day. He's not going to run away".

"Is that why you haven't told anyone all this before?"

"I mentioned parts of it to Mr. Frost Sir, but I wanted to get all the evidence before I jumped the gun. I think I have enough now Sir".

"Superintendent Gray finished the interview and Bell remained in the room, Summers seated opposite him. Gray went out and had a hushed conversation with Frost. He picked up the telephone in Summer's office and spoke in quiet tones to the Assistant Chief Constable who in turn, spoke to the Chief Constable at a civic dinner.

Half an hour later, the Assistant Chief Constable rang back and spoke to Gray. The conversation was short and to the point. Gray's face was serious.

"Very well Sir", he said. "I will tell him. Goodnight".

Gray ambled back into the interview room and sat down opposite Bell. He sighed heavily and offered the Detective a cigarette. He lit the cigarettes and blew smoke out of his mouth to make the atmosphere even thicker. He rubbed his forehead, then stubbed out his cigarette in anger. He seemed to be torn between loyalty and duty.

"Bell", he started. "I'm afraid I have to tell you that as from this moment, you are suspended from duty. You will not be permitted to enter this building until further notice, nor to communicate with any Police Officer about this case, with the exception of your Federation Representative. You will be informed of the progress of the investigation against you. I'm sorry. Can I have your warrant card?"

Harry Bell felt as though he had been felled with an axe. HE dropped his head forward and blinked. He shook his head from side to side and screwed his face up in anger. He felt dizzy and sick. He wanted to strike someone - anyone would do, just to rid himself of this frustration that had built up suddenly. An aching sensation made his head reel and he turned pale as sweat beads formed on his forehead beneath the lock of hair which had fallen forward.

"Bell, are you alright?", asked Gray, taking him by the shoulders and pushing his head between his open knees. "Bell", he called. "Bell, come on man, it isn't that bad".

The room was swimming and voices sounding far off, broke the silence, and the darkness began to lighten as Bell's senses returned. He felt strong hands gripping his shoulders and then lifting him into a fully sitting position on the hard chair. Someone was loosening his tie and unbuttoning his shirt collar. He reached up and wiped a hand across his damp forehead and blinked the perspiration out of his eyes. He took a deep breath and exhaled slowly.

"Are you alright now, Harry?", Gray's voice said.

Bell blinked and looked into the face of his Superintendent. A concerned expression on the man's face told Bell that Gray was worried. Worried about what was happening to one of the best Detectives he had on his staff.

"Fine", whispered Bell. "I'm alright now thank you Sir", he said.

"Look, I'll take you home myself Harry", said the Superintendent. "I don't like this any more than you do. But I have to do what I'm told as well you know. Things will work out alright, you wait and see. I'll follow up that Chandler angle and if there's any way of clearing you, I will".

Bell took his warrant card from his wallet and handed it to Gray. It was almost like resigning. He felt saddened and humiliated.

"Why don't you go away for a few days, Harry?", Gray advised as they drove home. "Why not go down and see that wife of yours, where is it - Sussex way?"

"I might do that, Sir", said Bell. "I reckon now is as good a time as any and I might get the chance of winning my wife back too - if I can get her away from that dragon of a mother".

"Well try to relax, Harry - Christ you need it man".

Gray dropped Bell outside the house.

"I'll have Peterson drive your car up tonight, and leave it here for you, alright?"

"Thank you Sir", said Bell, and he watched Gray drive away. "Pity we haven't got a few more bosses like that one", he said to himself as he watched the tail lights disappear.

Chapter 29

After a restless night's sleep, Bell messed about, cleaning and tidying the house. If he was going to try to bring Susan back, then he would have to have the place looking shipshape for her. He busied himself all morning, then, having lunched at the local cafe, he drove himself down towards the South coast.

Traffic was heavy and the going was slow and tedious. Still, there was no hurry. He had all the time in the world now. He was very concerned about his suspension from duty and he knew that he would remain so until the whole matter had been thoroughly investigated. Resignation was one thing, but suspension from duty, well - that was something different. Somehow, when a copper got suspended, the result of the enquiry never seemed to clear him completely and the smell of suspicion always stayed with him. People would point the accusing finger - 'there's the copper who got done for bribery'......and so on. It left a nasty taste in one's mouth.

The journey gave him an opportunity to analyse himself, and he searched his mind for the right words to say to Sue. He loved her just as much as ever, although he felt he would not be able to depend on her too much again in a crisis. She had proved herself to be too selfish in that respect. However, he was going to try to make amends himself, he decided, and that, if nothing else, should alter things to some extent.

It was six o'clock in the evening when he arrived at the little coastal resort and parked his car on the cliff top near the cottage. He switched off and made a point of not hurrying out of the car, in order to allow Sue time to come to greet him. She did not come out; neither did her mother. Bell opened his door and slammed it again then walked slowly up the garden path towards the front door. He knocked and a few seconds later Sue's mother opened it.

"What are you doing here?", she demanded.

"Why shouldn't I come here?", Bell replied, his resolve to be nice already weakening.

"Well, you haven't exactly been too bothered these last few weeks have you?", the woman said bitterly.

"I've not been in any position to come before", Bell answered, annoyance now showing in his voice.

"Well you're wasting your time coming here now anyway. Susan isn't here".

"What do you mean, she isn't here?"

"She went back to you only today. She tried to telephone you but there was no reply - as usual".

"When did she ring?"

"Several times last night. I suppose you were out having a good time".

"How has she gone?"

"She went on the coach. Should be there by now I should think. I don't really know what she sees in a man like you, I really don't. She wouldn't take any notice of me - I told her I did, I said, don't go back to that good-for-nothing Harry, he won't do you any good; but she would never listen".

"Good. It's about bloody time she saw things for herself instead of listening to you, you interfering old battle-axe. Now perhaps you'll leave us alone".

"Don't you speak to me like that my lad".

"Lad! Christ woman, you don't know what you're saying".

"I think you had better leave this house Harry, right now".

"Too bloody true I will", snorted Bell. "And good bloody riddance you old bitch".

Bell slammed out of the house and jumped into the car. The starter jammed and he felt such a fool sitting there, unable to start the thing. He got out and pushed the car about twenty yards to where the road sloped away, then jumped in and let it roll of its own accord. He switched on the ignition and engaged gear then bump-started it, then drove off, leaving a cloud of blue smoke behind him.

He drove to the sea front, parked the car, and went for a good stiff drink in the 'Seashell Tavern'. Over a steak he thought things over.

"So Susan is home", he mused. A thrill went through him. She must have given the matter considerable thought and come to the conclusion that their marriage was worth something after all. He was pleased, and ate his dinner with relish. It made up for the shock of being suspended. At least he would have his wife to go home to, and that was worth more than anything else now.

"Let the Police Force do what they will", he thought. "Let them throw the book at me, let them even sack me - Susan is my life from now on. I won't mind what they do, just so long as they don't drive her away from me again".

Bell finished his meal and went to the telephone. He put some change on the shelf and dialled his home number. He heard the telephone ring out for some seconds, and then his heart raced as the ringing stopped and he heard Susan's breath, heavy as if she had hurried from some other part of the house.

"Hello", she said. Her voice was soft and clear and heavenly, and Bell felt his legs go weak.

"Hello", she repeated. "Susan Bell here".

"Sue", breathed Bell. "Oh Sue, you're home".

"Harry - is that you?", she said, eagerly and Bell could detect the smile already upon her face.

""Welcome home darling", he said sincerely. "I'm glad you're back".

"Where are you Harry?", she asked. "When will you be home?"

"You'll never guess", he said. "I'm at your mother's - well not exactly at her house, she threw me out, but I'm in the town. I've just had a bite to eat and I'm just about to hit the motorway home. See you in about three hours sweetheart".

"Oh Harry, mind how you go. I'll be here when you arrive. I love you darling and I'll never go away from you, ever again".

"I love you too, Sue", Bell said softly, and with all the sincerity he could put into his tone.

"Harry?"

"Yes darling?"

"Are you on leave or something?"

"Something like that, pet", he replied. "Something like that".

The motorway was pretty clear and Bell tanked the old car along at its maximum speed as much as he could keep it up. He didn't bother if it didn't go any further than his front door, just so long as it got him home. Then, to hell with it, he'd buy a new one. He sang as he drove and he felt a different man. Already his depression was lifting fast and he saw his happiness returning once more. He was going home to his wife, and that was all that mattered.

Chapter 30

Bell was within a couple of miles from home. The siren of the large fire tender coming up fast behind him, sounded urgent. He pulled over and waved it on, then saw that there were two tenders. A little later, a Police car flashed past him, two tone horns blaring and blue light flashing.

"Must be a big fire somewhere", he thought. A second Police car flashed past him and Bell recognised the Scenes of Crime Officer sitting in the back.

He drove steadily on and saw the fire engines and the Police cars turn left up at the traffic lights. He turned into the same road a few seconds later. The emergency vehicles were out of sight. Bell drove on having dismissed the incident.

On reaching another turning where he wanted to turn left, he found the road blocked by barriers. Firemen seemed to be running about everywhere, and several Police vehicles were now in the vicinity, uniformed and plain clothes men were asking questions and Bell could see the glare from the fire over the tops of the vehicles. He also saw a house along the road, belching flames and smoke towards the sky. The house was like an inferno, and Bell realised that the brigade would be unable to do much to save the premises or contents. He began to panic - the house was in his own road, and although at first, he hadn't given it a thought, he realised too, that the fire was just about where his own house stood. He jumped out of his car and raced past the barricade and along the footpath, tripping over hoses and slipping on water. He weaved his way in and out of onlookers and firemen, and a Police Sergeant called him to stop. He continued and his heart raced. He felt the cold knife edge of panic as he discovered that the fire was indeed, his own home - now burning like the depths of hell, flames belching from every window and through the roof which had now collapsed. Firemen played hoses onto the roaring fire, but didn't seem to be doing any good at all. Bell tried to dash past them but a Policeman grabbed him.

"You can't go in there mate", the Officer said. "You'd never get in".

"That's my bloody house", barked Bell, struggling, going insane with fear and panic. "Where is my wife?"

"Your wife Sir", the Constable echoed.

"Yes, my wife", replied Bell desperately. "My wife was in there - did she get out?"

"Are you sure your wife was in there Sir?", asked the Officer, looking round for inspiration.

Bell looked at the man. He was new to the division. "It's the first time another copper has ever called me Sir", he thought. A woman hobbled over. It was his next door neighbour.

"His wife left him weeks ago, Constable", she said. "She went to her mother's down in Sussex. She wasn't in there. The poor man is delirious".

"She was in there", yelled Bell. "She came home today. I telephone her only three hours ago. She's in there I tell you". He struggled free and ran towards the hole where the front door had been. The Constable ran after him and pulled him back.

"You'll kill yourself if you go in there mate", he said.

"So what if I do?", shouted Bell, and then the house seemed to fold up and the walls caved in and showered them all with dust and ashes and burning timbers. The Constable dragged Bell away and took him to a car in the road.

"Sit in there a minute", he said. "Take things a bit easy".

Bell felt that sickening feeling creeping over him once more. His head began to pound and his heart tap-tapped like a woodpecker. His legs and arms felt weak, and a lump in his throat prevented him from swallowing.

"God, what have they done. What has happened......Why, why, why?", he cried, and the tears at last welled up in his tired eyes and trickled down his cheeks. He sobbed and wept bitterly, not caring who saw him. He cried like a baby, the built-up emotions of the recent weeks spouting from within his burdened soul, like the hot ashes shooting out of an erupting volcano. His heart felt as though it was tearing itself in half, and his stomach twisted with the agony running through his entire body. He shook as he sobbed, and the Police driver felt embarrassed and helpless. He let Bell cry it out, knowing that the grief within this man was something that had to be flushed out of his system and what better way than to be flushed by the tears of sorrow and the pain of lost love.

When Bell had cried all the tears that would come, he sat up and blew his nose. He looked back to the place where his home had once stood, and saw the blackened heap of rubble. He turned to an Inspector who was standing now beside the car. He was another new Inspector recently posted from headquarters.

"Any idea what happened?", Bell asked. "I mean, how did it start?"

"Explosion", said the Inspector.

"How?", said Bell.

"Don't know exactly", replied the Inspector. "May have been a bomb".

"A bomb! Have you got any leads on it?"

The Inspector turned towards Bell, realising at last that he was answering questions without even knowing to whom he was speaking.

"Who are you then?"

"I'm Detective Constable Bell Sir. That's my house".

The Inspector looked sharply at Bell and frowned. He saw the grief in the man's face and eyes.

"I'm sorry", he said. "I didn't know......yes, we do have a lead. Just a small one. Someone saw a large green Daimler car speed away just a few seconds before the place went up".

"Daimler did you say Sir?"

"Yes, does it mean anything to you?"

"I'm pretty certain it does Sir", said Bell thoughtfully.

Bell looked again towards the smouldering mass and saw the firemen rummaging about in the rubble. Someone shouted and two Detectives ran over to join the firemen. They poked about for a while in a corner, then sent for the Detective Chief Inspector who had arrived only a few minutes earlier. Frost got out of his car and stumbled over the remains of the front garden and joined the men by torchlight in the rubble. Heads nodded, and Bell knew what they had found. He didn't want to see. He got out of the Police car and stumbled away up the road out of the way of the onlookers, then he collapsed against a wall and heaved and was violently sick. They had destroyed him completely - they had destroyed his career and now they had taken his wife from him and from life itself - and now there was nothing left.

Chapter 31

Superintendent Gray had been busy. He had sifted all the facts from Bell's report and had complimented the Detective in his absence, for such a comprehensive well written account. The evidence available was certainly good enough to swear out a warrant for Chandler's arrest. Pity they hadn't held on to the man the previous night when he was supposed to have gone to the Police Station to make a statement. He just hadn't turned up, but the following morning, a letter had been delivered by a young lad by hand, addressed to the Officer In Charge. It was a written statement, signed C. Wilkins, and alleged all the offenses of blackmail which he claimed Bell had committed during the previous nine months. A letter accompanied the statement and said that Wilkins had not gone to the Police Station as arranged because he was too frightened, but hoped that the enclosed statement would suffice.

Gray had wasted no time at all in getting a warrant out for Chandler's arrest and had sent a team of Detectives to watch the house where Bell had followed the man previously. The Detectives watched in vain all day.

William Chandler, alias Charles Wilkins, properly known as Henry Cleaver, had got word of the move and was preparing to vacate the town. He had driven to his office in the heart of town and telephoned his contacts in order to arrange a flight on a private aircraft across the channel. He had planned to spend several months abroad before returning to recoup his losses and re-establish himself in some other town or city.

Cursing Bell for his stubbornness, he had sworn to ruin him completely. He was pleased that he had at least been responsible for Bell's suspension from duty and possible dismissal from the Force - even a possible prison sentence. He was a master of intrigue and frame-ups were his speciality. Bell had fallen into his hands so easily; and the allegation of blackmail, backed up by the photograph of misconduct, and the recent adverse press account of Bell's behaviour which had resulted in the death of Rodway, would surely add up to Bell's final downfall as a copper.

"At least he won't be on my back again", Chandler had sneered. But there was one more thing he had to do to teach the man a lesson. He had to show Bell that when Chandler calls for action, he expects to get it. The final job, he would carry out himself - something that he never normally did - but this time it was different.

And so it was, that at nine o'clock on that fateful evening, William Chandler had pulled up outside Bell's home, knowing that Mrs. Bell had left her husband, or at least, had gone away. The house would be empty and he knew that Bell's total wealth reposed within its four walls. He was going to deprive the man of all he possessed.

Chandler had climbed out of the big Daimler, the engine still ticking over silently. A bottle of petrol with a single stick of gelignite taped to it, sprouted a rag taper from the neck. He had strolled up to the front window and looked up and down the street, lifted the bottle and lit the end of the taper with a cigarette lighter, and thrown the bomb through the downstairs front window. He had run back up the drive and jumped into his car. The nosey neighbour had watched from behind her heavy curtains and seen him get into the car and drive away.

The explosion, seconds later, had rocked the house and the woman had seen the great ball of flame spread across the front garden, then watched as it was sucked back through the window frame. Within minutes, the entire house was burning uncontrollably.

Chapter 32

Now Chandler hurried through his final arrangements and made a last telephone call from the public call box on the road to the private flying club just outside Dunstley. It was here that an observant patrol car driver spotted the car and relayed the information by radio to control. The 'Attention message' had been flashed to all patrols earlier that night when it had been found that Chandler was not at his home and would not be likely to return. Now, within the knowledge that he might also be responsible for blowing up a fellow policeman's home, all patrols were very much on the alert of the car.

The Constable noted the number and location and saw the big man in a telephone kiosk. He kept the man under observations and waited for assistance. Chandler spotted him as he came out of the kiosk. He walked calmly towards his car then, as if sensing that he was about to be arrested, turned and ran for the cover of the trees at the foot of the sloping downs which encircled the flying club. He dashed along the leafy path, keeping to the shadows as much as possible. The patrol car driver sprinted after him and almost caught him. He would have succeeded had it not been for the wet leaves and grass. He slipped and tumbled headlong into a bramble bush, scratching his face and hands as he fell. Chandler took advantage of the Officer's mishap and veered off in another direction.

The four cars hurrying to the scene from different directions, all came across the abandoned Daimler at once. The patrol car, also empty, stood a few yards away from it. The Officers looked at each other, then at the hills and saw a figure emerging from the shadows, blood trickling down his face. The patrolman shouted to them and pointed.

"I don't know what you think, but he was making a telephone call when I saw him. He spotted me and made off up that way. I would think he's making for the flying club".

A Detective Sergeant and two Constables in a plain car sped off along the road towards the main entrance to the flying club. A few minutes later, they turned into the muddy driveway and sped up the long, bumpy road to the hangars and club house. A small Cherokee aircraft was warming up on the approach to the taxi-way, its pilot sitting at the controls. He was scanning the road as if expecting someone to arrive at any moment. He jumped down from the cockpit and went towards the plain car.

"All ready to go guv'nor", he said, putting his head in through the open window. He saw the Officers and realised that he had slipped up. Fear made him withdraw quickly.

"Stop - we're Police Officers", called the Sergeant, and the man stopped dead in his tracks.

"Is that your aircraft?", the Sergeant demanded, getting out of the car and moving towards the pilot.

"Yes", said the man weakly.

"And where exactly are you going at this time of night?"

"No where".

"Oh come now, you just told us you were all ready to go. Where?"

"No where - just testing the engines".

"At eleven o'clock at night?"

"Why not?"

There was movement over the hill and a figure appeared out of the shadows. The man ran towards the aircraft, panting and staggering. The pilot started to shout, but the Sergeant anticipated such a move and grabbed him, putting his hand across the man's mouth.

"Get him", he whispered to his colleagues who ran forward to meet the newcomer.

"This way Guv', quick", said one of the Constables, using a bit of initiative in the darkness.

"The bleedin' law's after me", called the exhausted Chandler. "We'll have to get off right away........". He suddenly stopped and realised that the two men in front of him were not his men. The uniforms showed up in the darkness. Chandler turned as if to run again, but the two Constables grabbed him and held him still.

"Alright mister, the game is over. You are under arrest".

"What for?", asked Chandler indignantly.

"We have a warrant Mr. Chandler".

Chandler did not struggle. He knew that the game was up and there was no way out of the predicament, not for the moment anyway. His lawyer would have to do all the thinking from now on - he would do his best to get Chandler off, if he could.

Chapter 33

No one really knew where Bell went after the fire. He just sort of disappeared. He was gone for three days and nights. He hardly knew himself, where he went or what he was doing. The night turned into an epic of torment, and his mind refused to register the situation or the events which took place about him. He walked until he collapsed, somewhere on waste ground. He awoke the next morning and wandered around again, all day, bumping into people on the crowded footpaths and walking across the busy roads, causing traffic to screech to unscheduled halts amid the cursing of agitated drivers. The days merged into night and his mind became a confusion of thoughts and gibberish. Pictures flashed in his head, like a jerky cinema screen - fire - Chandler - Penny Whiteman - a bundle of bank notes - Frost - smoke - Ruby - Susan - and cloudy reminiscences of people and events; and all the time, the hammering inside and the sweat soaking his aching body. Like a Zombie he staggered anywhere, he knew not where, nor why, until finally he stopped, blinked, and stared into the ugly, hard faces of leather jacketed cowboys, chains and studs decorating their jackets. Bell was aware at last, of himself and of his surroundings on open park-like land near the centre of the town. The place was the favoured haunt of winos, low class prostitutes and mugging teams. Somehow, he had ended up right there, amid the people he distrusted and disliked the most - almost one of them now, unshaven, unwashed, clothes dirty and creased, giving that slept-in appearance. His eyes were bloodshot, staring and wild, and his finger nails grubby. He stared into the faces of the gang of youths who had more reason than anyone to hate him, for wasn't he the copper who shot their leader?

Bell sensed the first blow but was incapable of defending himself. The bottle landed across the side of his head, splitting it wide open. He staggered and felt a boot in his back, shoving him forward. He dropped on hands and knees in time to meet a boot swinging up under his chin, and he tasted the blood from the split tongue between his teeth. A piece of wood struck him across the back, and in the midst of all the blows, he heard them chanting "Fuzz, Fuzz, Fuzz, Fuzz.....".

He rolled and squirmed as the blows continued to mark him; and he found himself looking helplessly into the eyes of passers-by. Some stopped and watched, others just carried on, unconcerned, not wanting to get involved. He felt himself being kicked over and over like a football, until he rolled down an embankment and felt the cool touch of water as his left leg and arm hung loosely to one side. He lay on his back, half in and half out of the stream. The world closed in on him, and he prayed that he was going to die just so long as he could be with Susan - and then there was blackness and silence..........

Chapter 34

Chandler had been put up for identification and picked out without hesitation by the neighbour who had seen him throw the bomb into Bell's house.

"That's the man", she had said, raising her voice emotionally; "that's the murdering swine".

"That'll do", said the Inspector in charge. "Thank you madam", and the woman had been led out.

Bill Peterson had also picked him out as the man he had seen in the 'Dick Turpin' public house after Don Broadman and the man in the blazer had hidden the stolen lorry.

The whole works had been blown, and property worth several thousand pounds had been recovered. Altogether no less than twenty five people had been roped in and charged with crimes varying from handling stolen property, to conspiracy to demand money with menace, and even arson and murder. William Chandler had been charged by Superintendent Gray, and the Magistrates had ordered a remand in custody for the key men in the organisation. Others were allowed bail. Even Marshall had been tied in with Chandler's operations, and had been arrested and charged with unlawfully administering drugs to Bell and offenses of conspiring with Chandler, to steal.

Harry Bell sat up in his hospital bed, very sore and very lonely. He had nothing much to live for, or so it seemed. His face was scarred and showed fifteen stitches where it had been ripped open by the bottle in the park. His body was a mass of abrasions and bruises, and his left arm broken below the elbow. He felt miserable.

Superintendent Gray, Frost, and even the Chief Constable himself, had been shocked on hearing of his condition. The night beat Officer had been directed to where he lay, by a rare, public spirited citizen who had then disappeared just as fast. He had been rushed by ambulance to the hospital for emergency treatment, and gentle hands had bathed and cleansed his battered body. His troubled mind had been eased with the aid of proper sedatives; and efficient professional hands had nursed him through the week long fight for recovery. Bell had been unaware of the visits he had received during that week. His Chiefs had been to see him, and a Detective sat constantly by his bedside, lest he should say anything which would indicate the cause of his injuries. Bell remembered nothing at all.

The West Indian Ward Sister came into his room, her white teeth shining as she beamed a happy smile at him.

"I have a visitor for you, Mr. Bell", she said.

Bell raised his eyes from the white sheet at which he had been staring for the past twenty minutes or so.

"Oh", he said. "Who is it then?", his voice sounded flat and disinterested.

"It's me", said a rich, deep tanned voice, and Ruby walked into the room. She smiled at the Sister and walked over to Bell. She bent over and kissed him, ever so lightly, on the forehead. "Hello Harry", she oozed.

"Ruby!", Bell exclaimed, surprised that she should come to visit him. "What are you doing here?"

"I came to see you Harry", Ruby said. "Don't you like that?"

"Sure - it's great to see you Ruby, but right now - I don't know what I do want". He seemed to be embarrassed, and felt awkward. He was more than conscious of his appearance, his face stitched and swollen and bruised.

Ruby took his free hand and held it gently. She looked him in the eye and smiled softly. "Poor Harry", she breathed. "What have they done to you". She blinked her damp eyes dry, and sat on the bed beside him. Bell said nothing, but she saw him biting into his lower lip.

"It's good to see you Harry my sweet", she said. "Are you pleased I came?"

"Sure...... Yes, I guess so", he paused, then, "yes, of course I am, baby".

"Still uncertain eh, Harry? Well never mind. I only came to see how you were. I have been worried about you and, well, I guess I owe you something. It's good to see you on the mend Harry man".

"Thanks Ruby", Bell winced. He moved to a more comfortable position then, for the first time in ages, smiled - just a little - but it was smile.

"Hey, that's better", Ruby remarked. "You see, I make you smile already - that's good eh?"

They talked, and Ruby held his hand all the time. She still looked good and Bell felt something of a bond between them. She could never replace Susan, that he knew, but there was at least something comforting about her - something that made him feel relaxed.

Ruby stayed for half an hour and then the Ward Sister insisted that it was time for Bell to rest. He would be having important Police visitors later, and he must not be allowed to get too tired.

Gray came in person that evening, and spoke to Bell. He was, he said, pleased to see Bell looking so much better and on the mend. There were a lot of formalities to go through and statements to sign besides a further talk about his injuries. Bell did not discuss his house or anything connected with it. What could he tell anyway?

"You will be out of hospital next week, I understand", said Gray. "I think we shall be able to wrap up this business about your suspension then".

"Oh!", commented Bell. "What has happened about that then, Sir?"

"Well, we have fully investigated the whole affair. Chandler had admitted that he set you up. Incidentally, we have charged him with setting fire to your house and with the murder of your....."

"My wife Sir?", interrupted Bell.

"Well, yes Harry. I'm sorry about that - I really am".

"Thank you Sir", said Bell, flatly. "I guess it's all part of the job". Bitterness reflected brazenly in his tone. Gray seemed a little embarrassed now.

"Am I in the clear then, Sir?" Bell said at last. "Do I get my warrant card back?"

"We'll discuss that next week, when you feel stronger, but just for your peace of mind, yes, you are to be reinstated".

"Good", said Bell.

Gray was thoughtful for while. He seemed a little troubled, as if trying to make up his mind to say something, yet could not find the right words. Finally, he broke the awkward silence.

"Harry", he said. "You have had a damned rough time. You have been through more in the last few months than most men go through in their whole service. I think you should take things easy for a while - you know, slow down, take more time off and all that. C.I.D. work is demanding as you well know, and I think a spell back in uniform, working straight shifts and getting regular time off will do you good. How do you feel about a transfer to uniform, Harry?"

Bell was astounded. He didn't like the suggestion at all. He was a Detective, and a bloody good Detective at that. He had no inclination to go back to uniform duties. He was a Detective and had grown accustomed to the ways of the C.I.D. He had the utmost respect for his uniformed colleagues - certainly, they were the backbone of the Police Service, but he just didn't feel the call of that side of the job. Anyway, now that he didn't have Susan to go home to, how the hell was he going to spend all that spare time if he went back into uniform?

"Well Harry, what do you think?"

"Sir, I can't go back to uniform duties - you should know that".

"Of course you can Harry. It need not be for too long. Just long enough for you to get yourself straightened out. You'll need plenty of spare time and you'll need to take work a little slower and steadier. Let someone else do the worrying for a change - you know it makes sense Harry".

"No Sir", replied Bell, stubbornly. "I won't go back to uniform".

"What if we say you must - the Chief can do that you know, any time he wants to. He can order you to go back into uniform. After all a P.C.'s job is just as interesting as yours, only he deals with a different sort of problem".

"I don't want to be a P.C. Sir".

"Well Harry", the Superintendent went on "it isn't up to me. I'll tell the Chief how you feel". He felt frustrated and somehow disloyal to his subordinate, but he also felt he had to do something to make amends.

"Thank you Sir", said Bell, closing his eyes.

Superintendent Gray tiptoed out of the ward and thanked the Sister. He was concerned deeply for Bell's future. He didn't want to lose a good Detective, but at the same time, he realised that if Bell continued as a C.I.D. man, he would soon crack up altogether. He could not go on as he had been, and he would only get himself more and more involved in his work now that he didn't have a wife to go home to at all. A transfer to uniform was the only way, and yet, such a move might drive him right out of the service altogether - that must be avoided at all costs. Men like Bell were too useful and they were few and far between, these days.

Chapter 35

The large square table in the Chief Constable's office was littered with papers. Service documents, personal records sheet, and a whole assortment of letters of appreciation all relating to Detective Constable Bell. The Chief Constable held the record sheet in his hands. Gray sat opposite tim, pipe smouldering in his strong grip, and the Assistant Chief Constable looked on from a spot by the window.

"You have told him that he will be reinstated, Mr. Gray?" said the Chief.

"Yes Sir".

"And what do you think we ought to do about these other matters?"

"You mean the shooting incident Sir?"

"That, and this sex orgy thing".

"I think that was a flash in the pan if anything Sir. He was put up for that one. The shooting, I think, shows him in his most favourable light Sir. If he had not taken such quick and decisive action - I would have been dead. I think that is highly commendable of the man".

"Yes, we all know that Gray", said the Chief, irritably, "but the thing that counts is what the public think. I can't have the public thinking that I have men on my force who will shoot to kill every time someone goes a bit berserk with a gun".

"But Sir", went on Gray. "He saved my life. Doesn't that mean more than a bit of publicity. You know the press Sir. They'll make a sensation of anything that concerns the police - even over a dispute about a radar trap".

"Mr. Gray, I am aware of the press methods used in this present age, but I must show the public that I have done something to protect them from a repetition of such a tragedy".

"Alright Sir, what do you suggest?"

"Put him back in uniform!", the Assistant Chief Constable declared from over by the window. "The man should be back in uniform".

"That's what you want Sir?", said Gray. "Alright - you will lose him".

"What do you mean?", said the Chief, raising his bushy eyebrows.

"If you put him back as a uniform P.C., he will resign. He told me so".

"Bluff", guffawed the Assistant Chief.

"Are you prepared to call that bluff then Sir?", said Gray; "bear in mind that we are already two hundred men under strength in this force. We can't afford to go chucking men like Bell away, simply to satisfy a public criticism".

"You're right Gray - we can't", said the Chief Constable. "But what do we do then? We can't allow him to drive himself any more in C.I.D. We are agreed that to continue in that branch would break him up completely and he would end up perhaps in some mental hospital within six months, after his experience. Yet, if we remove him to uniform as a P.C., he'll resign and that would be just as much a loss to us and to the public who deserve the best policemen we can give them".

There was a silence and the three men thought about the problem in hand. The Assistant Chief picked up the files and studied them. He raised his brows from time to time as he read, for the first time, of the career of Harry Bell. Eleven commendations in ten years. Many years in C.I.D. - courses in just about every aspect of Crime detection. Perfect record with the exception of one or two minor complaints against him, but then, that was the hallmark of a good copper - shows at least that he is doing his job. A copper who never gets a complaint made against him, just isn't getting about enough.

"Well Mr. Gray", the Chief said at last. "He is your man. What do you suggest?"

Gray sat upright and took his pipe out of his mouth. He smoothed his tie and sighed heavily.

"There is a way Sir", he said calmly. "I think it would save the day. It would save face, achieve your aim to put him back into uniform, and ensure that he doesn't resign. Everyone including Bell himself, should be happy". He paused to let his remarks sink in.

"Well", said the Chief, impatiently. "What is it then?"

"You could promote him Sir", said Gray seriously.

"Promote him!", exclaimed the Assistant Chief.

"Yes Sir - promote him. He is qualified and would make a fine Sergeant. He couldn't argue with that and it is policy to transfer from branch to branch on promotion. He deserves it and should have been made up years ago".

"Qualified?", queried the Chief. "Has he passed the examinations then?"

"Good Lord, yes Sir - five years ago", replied Gray. "It is in his records Sir".

"Well, so he has", said the Chief, eyeing the documents in front of him.

"Hmmm, I'm not sure", said the Assistant Chief, doubtfully.

"Why not?", demanded the Chief.

"Well Sir, he has been in a bit of bother lately hasn't he? It might be a bad thing to promote a man on top of all that - bad example".

"He has been cleared of that", said Gray impatiently. "He's done no more than his job and I would have been annoyed if he hadn't".

"I agree with Mr. Gray", said the Chief. "When is Bell back on duty?"

"Three days time Sir. Starts Monday morning".

"Good. Have him in my office then, eleven o'clock. I'm going to promote him. Jolly good idea Mr. Gray, what?"

"Thank you Sir", said Gray, smiling. He was grateful and pleased that he had been responsible for the furtherance of Bell's career thus far. "Bell will be a fine Sergeant", he said.

Chapter 36

Sergeant Harry Bell stepped out of the Chief Constable's office onto the landing of the old building. The floor shone brightly, and an Inspector walked awkwardly past, a cup of tea in his hand. He glanced at Bell and nodded.

"Alright then?", he whispered, smiling.

"Yes thanks Sir", replied Bell, without returning the smile. He walked along the hall and began to go down the stairs to the ground floor.

Superintendent Gray rushed down the stairs behind him.

"Harry", he called. Bell stopped and turned. "Congratulations Harry", Gray said. "I really am pleased for you".

"Thank you Sir", said Bell.

"Well, how does it feel to be a Sergeant?"

"I still feel like Harry Bell Sir".

"Yes, but don't you feel you have achieved something too, Harry?"

"Have I Sir? Have I achieved something - or has the Chief?"

"I don't follow you Harry".

"I think you do Sir", replied Bell, his face serious, hard as ever.

"Look Harry, you've made it man. Can't you accept that. You've got on to the ladder of success. You're over the hardest step now Harry".

"Yes Sir".

Gray was disappointed at Bell's response. He had wanted the man to feel good about his promotion, but as usual, Bell had seen through the plan and frustrated the issue. He felt had about it now.

"Well congratulations anyway". Gray turned to go back upstairs to his office.

"Mr. Gray Sir", Bell called softly. Gray turned this time to face Bell.

"Thank you Sir", Bell said. "I appreciate what you did".

"Me? I've done nothing Harry".

"Thanks anyway Sir", and Bell smiled, a friendly smile.

Half an hour later, Bell slipped the white envelope into the letter box outside the headquarters. He climbed once more into his old car and drove slowly to the cemetery. He parked and walked reverently through the lines of graves, flowers blooming, some actually growing, others displayed in elaborate pots. He moved silently and slowly until he stopped beside a mound of fresh earth. The wreaths were still quite fresh and laid in profusion over the grave into which his whole purpose in life had been lowered just a few days before.

Bell stood, head bowed and hands joined loosely together in front of him. He looked down at the flowers and saw a card, ink now smearing from the simple words "with fond memories of our daughter". Another card, type written "From Harry".

He closed his eyes and believed that he could see Susan's face gazing up at him from the earth. He felt the first tear forcing its way under his eyelid, and he blinked, allowing the drop to trickle down his hard, tired face, then more tears gently flowed and he shook with the emotion that would not leave him. He knelt down and took a flower in his hands and lifted it to his wet lips. He kissed the bloom and murmured a prayer.

"Forgive me Sue", he whispered. "Forgive me", and he wept from his inner soul and dampened the flower still in his hands. Then he stood up, dried his eyes and walked away.

The simple white envelope on the Chief Constable's desk the following morning, was on top of the pile of letters addressed personally to him. The Chief Constable opened the envelope and withdrew the plain sheet of paper. He read and dropped the letter on his desk. He looked up at the ceiling, fists clenched, and sighed.

"Gray", he said over the telephone. "Come in here will you please?"

Superintendent Gray read the print on the clean white sheet of paper, and cursed. He shook his head from side to side, and pursed his lips. He thought for a while as if trying to think of a good enough reason for the decision, and sighed again.

"I suppose we can't really blame him Sir", he said. "He was a good copper. A born Detective - straight as they come, yet hard enough for the best of 'em".

"So we've lost him after all Gray", said the Chief. "You said he wouldn't resign. Well he has!"

"Yes Sir", said Gray, sadly. "He's finished".

Epilogue

They didn't know what caused the accident. Bell was found slumped at the wheel of his car, the bonnet buried deep under the back of a huge continental trailer. He was still clutching a single bloom which looked like it had come from a wreath. His face was still wet with fresh tears. Perhaps his prayer had been answered. Perhaps he was now with Susan - perhaps that was how it was meant to end........

END